CHAPTER ONE

Driving the elderly car which was all she could now afford, Libby Garfield's hands were clamped around the steering-wheel. Never in a million years would she have guessed she would be visiting the boarding school where she had once been secretary. She would never have gone to the unveiling ceremony of the plaque in memory of her husband, Grant, if his grandmother, Mary Garfield, hadn't asked her to drive.

'Libby, dear,' Mary said gently, 'I know what's to come will be very painful, but do try to relax. This is something neither of us expected to happen, least of all me. A grandson dying before you isn't something one imagines will ever happen. I expect, like me, you thought Grant would stop dashing off to war zones once you were married.'

'Oh, he made it very plain that wouldn't happen.'

Libby thought her tone was normal, but Mary was observant, and had heard the slight hardness in her voice.

'You know, he did love you, in his odd way. He told me he was instantly attracted to you because you didn't fawn around him when he went to that Old Boys' do.'

'That made me yet another challenge for

1

him. I didn't fawn around him because I didn't know who he was.'

'Would it have lasted?' Mary asked, then hastily grabbed the door handle as Libby took a corner too sharply.

Although knowing what her elderly companion was getting at, Libby pretended not to understand, so giving herself time to think. 'His career as a war correspondent you mean? Grant said he wanted to die with his boots on and he certainly did that,' she said grimly, remembering the gory details published in newspapers and the photographs. Hadn't the media any thought for the family and friends? That he was one of them seemed to make them more eager to make a big thing of it. She was called the grieving child-widow. Child indeed! She was twenty.

Mary nodded, for she, too, had been pestered, reporters and camera men jostling outside her door. Knowing Grant and his domineering ways, she had hoped Libby would soften him so they would live happily, nothing like her own marriage. Staring at the passing countryside, Mary sighed. If she wanted to remember her husband who had died five years previously, she had only to look at Grant.

'I was interested in art, but it was thought a waste of time,' she said so softly that Libby knew it was a voiced thought, a recalling.

'I didn't know that.' She glanced at her watch. 'We're going to arrive early and don't relish having sympathy poured over me like black treacle for a minute longer than I can help. So shall I stop at a convenient place and we can stretch our legs?'

Parking on the verge near a footpath sign, they walked in companionable silence over a stubble field for a few minutes, each thinking about the other, their sorrow, and in Mary's case, the difference Grant's death would make to the young girl beside her. Six months on, the media still pestered Libby, wanting to know how she was dealing with her life as a tragic young widow.

Stopping at a five-barred gate, they leaned on it, staring down at the large sprawl of the school's old buildings in the valley below.

'Would you go back there if they asked you?' Mary asked.

'No! And it's not what you think. Grant's ghost doesn't follow me around. He might have enjoyed his school days there, but to me it was just a job. It's strange really, but some of him has rubbed off on me. I was always a little apprehensive about life. But now . . .' Libby laughed.

Mary had to reach up to put her arm around Libby's slim shoulders for she was above average height.

'But I did wonder, seeing how much he changed you, the clothes, hairstyle, the parties, all of which I felt weren't truly you. You can tell me it's none of my business, but why did you marry him? Did he, as they say, sweep you off your feet?'

'Yes, in a way he did. I was naïve, inexperienced.'

Glancing at her, Mary could see from the way Libby's lips were clamped together, that she was on the point of saying more but felt she couldn't, or didn't want to.

'I've no illusions about my grandson. He was too much like my husband for me to think him an angel. Although we were comfortably off, Charles kept me short of money. He took pleasure in me going cap in hand asking for money to buy the smallest thing. But nevertheless, by careful budgeting, I eventually managed to save enough to pay for art lessons.'

As she trailed off, Libby finished the sentence with, 'But Charles stopped you going. So why didn't you take it up when he died?'

'This is why.'

Mary held up her hands, fingers now knotted by arthritis.

'So tell me, what did Grant stop you doing?'

'I suppose he stopped me being myself.'

'He hasn't permanently stopped you,' Mary responded firmly. 'You only had a short time together and for some of that he was away, so basically you're still the young girl you were before you married. So, if I was your fairy godmother and could give you a wish, what would you like to be or do?'

4

Turning to lean her back against the gate, Libby looked up at the sky. 'I'd like to live in the country and . . .' She frowned. What could she possibly do in the country? Keep goats? Run a guest house? But she hadn't any money. Grant had used credit cards with no thought to the mounting debt. If it hadn't been for Mary settling the huge accounts . . .

As tears slid down Libby's cheeks, Mary took her in her arms, murmuring conventional words of comfort.

*   *   *

Almost twelve months on, Libby's first sighting of Sanctuary Wood was from the top of the hill on the opposite side of the valley. Stopping her car, she got out, surprised as a gust of wind tousled her short, dark hair.

This was her first glimpse of the wood which was to be both her place of work and home. It had been Mary's brainchild, her money which had bought the small group of timber-built lodges which had been holiday lets. But their purpose now was different, a small colony for artists and musicians to have peace and quiet.

Libby's shoulders were hunched more in excitement than against the wind. Deliberately, she had refused to be involved in the planning and alterations for she knew this was Mary's way of helping. But everything was now ready, the four men were due the next day and Libby knew it was up to her to make Sanctuary Wood work. Besides being a great opportunity to stand on her own two feet again, away from her family, she owed it to Mary.

'You lost or something?'

Startled, Libby turned as a battered grey van which had come up the hill towards her, slowed down.

'It might be a grand view for the moment, but you mark my words, from the look of yonder clouds, we're in for a right old storm before long.'

'Thanks.' She smiled ruefully. 'I'm afraid I hadn't noticed.'

'Well, you wouldn't, you not being local! Come far, have you?'

Her questioner was now looking at her closely through his wound-down window, the mud-caked glass having prevented him seeing her clearly. The questioning immediately had her on her guard, for Mary had advised her to say nothing of her past to anyone, otherwise the media would be skulking in the wood, taking photographs, pestering anyone who would talk to them.

Hurriedly getting into her car, she slammed the door to cut off his next question. She started the engine, but flustered by this unexpected encounter, the car did not move smoothly away but kangaroo hopped.

She gained control of herself and the car.

How silly! He couldn't possibly have recognised her. Gone was the long, dyed-blonde hair Grant had insisted upon. Gone, too, the glamorous clothes. What a relief it had been to get back her former clothes from the friend she had left them with before the wedding. It was almost as if she'd had a premonition . . .

Trying to beat the advancing rain, Libby drove so fast she almost missed the turning on to the roughly-stoned track leading to the wood. Ominous clouds were now turning the early May afternoon into twilight and she switched on the headlights just in time to see a weathered gate barring her way. Hurrying to open it, a freshly-painted board on it warned, *No vehicles allowed in the wood! Please use carpark and shut gate.*

As the first heavy raindrops fell, Libby didn't waste time parking neatly on the small, level area beyond the gate. She could do that early the following morning.

Mary, having shown her a plan of the site, Libby knew the way to her new home, Keeper's Lodge, which had been built on the site of an old gamekeeper's cottage. Awkwardly holding a box of groceries, she hurried along the path wending its way through large beech and oaks. She eagerly unlocked the door.

Once inside, she turned right, going into the large kitchen where every day she was to cook an evening meal for the four men who each had a small, isolated lodge deep in the wood. The idea was that they should have the peace they needed, but to avoid loneliness turning into despair, they would all share a meal at Keeper's Lodge every evening.

As the wind drove the rain against the window, Libby shivered. What she needed was a hot drink! Waiting for the kettle to boil, she was glad to see that all the kitchen equipment was new, up-to-date. Then, cradling a mug of coffee, she explored the rest of her home, her bolt hole.

Another door led to a small storeroom containing spare light bulbs, cleaning materials and tools, the latter already well-used, presumably by Mr Jones who came in a few days a week to do odd jobs and look after the wood. Keeping him on had been part of the deal when Mary had bought Sanctuary Wood, for he had looked after it for years. She had smiled when she had told Libby.

'He likes to be called Mr Jones, but, Libby dear, have you decided what you'll be called? In the brochure, I've not mentioned you by name.'

'Mary, I hope you don't mind, but I've reverted to my maiden name, Weston. But I hope the atmosphere will be so relaxed that we'll all be on first-name terms, except of course for Mr Jones!'

The rain having eased, Libby unloaded the

car, and was soon happily putting her clothes and a few personal possessions away in the small bedroom, including her last birthday present from Grant, a small silver trinket box decorated with an elaborate E for Elizabeth, her given name.

Flopping down on the comfortable green sofa, she smiled. Sanctuary Wood, as a place of escape, would do very nicely. Outwardly, she had reverted to what she had looked like before she had married and as far as the four men were concerned, she was a single girl, looking for a change from her previous job as a school secretary.

It was the sound of a powerful motorbike which brought her to her feet. Surely the wood wasn't used by lads intent on gouging tracks between the trees? Careless of her own safety and the drizzle, she ran out, pausing briefly to gauge the direction of the engine's roar.

'This is private property!' she shouted to the leather-clad, helmeted figure bending over the panniers at the rear of the machine.

Thinking he might be intending on camping in the woods, she hurried forward. 'You can't stop here.'

As he slowly straightened, fear trickled down her spine. Tall, broad shouldered, he was faceless behind the helmet's visor. 'There's no need to stand there like a frightened rabbit.' His deep voice was slightly muffled as he removed his helmet. 'When you say I can't stop here, did you mean I've parked in the wrong place? Or is it because I've arrived a day early? If Oak Lodge isn't quite ready, I don't mind. I'm used to roughing it,' he said, easing off a bulky backpack.

It was only as he took off his right gauntlet and came towards her that Libby realised she had been standing looking at him as though he had come from Mars.

'Hi, I'm Jake Vaunt. You must be Matron, seeing we eat one square meal a day and bring our laundry on time.'

Although he held out his hand, he stopped far enough away from her so his arm was outstretched. Their handshake was brief, a courtesy. She smiled. She liked that. He wasn't like so many men coming as close as possible, forcing intimacy.

'I would prefer if you called me Libby, not Matron,' she said lightly, looking up at the first arrival.

Grant had often said that his safety in a war zone depended on looking someone in the face, summing them up. But he hadn't told her what to deduce from a tanned, square-jawed face with granite-grey eyes! She couldn't tell Jake Vaunt's hair colour because it was closely cropped, but from the darkness of his eyebrows and lashes, his hair would be similar.

'Were you previously in the police, used to noting every detail of a face?'

There was no humour in his question, just

plain enquiry.

'No . . . I'm sorry . . . I didn't mean to . . . it was just I wasn't expecting anyone.'

'I won't be needing an evening meal.' He turned back to the motorbike. 'I've brought enough food.'

Nonplussed, she watched as he quickly unpacked the panniers.

'There's no need to hang about, you're getting wet.'

She winced at the slight impatience in his voice. She must indeed look like a rabbit, too scared to move.

'You know your way then?'

'Yes. I'm in Oak. It's on the plan I was sent. I'll see you tomorrow evening.'

Ignoring the path, he took a short cut through the trees and as Libby returned to Keeper's Lodge, she was frowning. This wasn't at all how she had planned to welcome the men. They might be wanting solitude but she hadn't expected such . . . she searched for the right word for Jake Vaunt . . . aloofness.

That night, sleeping deeply, she was unaware she had silenced her alarm clock. It was a sharp rapping on her bedroom window which snapped her awake, fright taking her from prone to upright by the bed in a split second. The strength of the daylight had her muttering a dismayed, 'Oh, no!' as she hurried to the window, opening the curtains just sufficiently to peer out.

'A bad hangover?'

Having seen the movement, her visitor stood there smiling. Although her view was limited, she could see this man wasn't Jake for he was much older, shorter, well-rounded and wearing a flowery shirt which she guessed Jake would only have used to clean his motorbike! So which of the other three was this latest arrival?

'Give me a minute,' she called back.

Dressing quickly, she was annoyed with herself. What a negative impression she had made on the first two men, not at all like the cool efficiency she had planned! She used her fingers to rake her hair tidy as she opened the door on to the veranda.

'I'm Libby Weston,' she began, 'I'm so sorry I overslept.'

'There's no need to apologise. I believe country air does the most horrible things to one's constitution.' Shuddering in a comical, exaggerated manner, her visitor peered past her. 'I know we've not to treat this place like a hotel, but I'm dying for a cup of tea!'

'Come in, I was going to make one anyway.'

As he sat down, arms folded, inspecting the kitchen, she surmised this man was the opposite of Jake in more than just dress. He liked company, in which case, why had he come to Sanctuary Wood?

'Like the first day of term, rules are relaxed, but tomorrow we play strictly by the book,' she warned, busying herself with kettle, toaster and the other things needed for breakfast.

Although well aware he was watching, she avoided eye contact. She had to make him understand that she was immune to charm.

'You're frowning,' he accused lightly. 'Don't tell me you're one of those women who thinks a man should actually do things in the kitchen, like helping you?'

'You're certainly going to have to do things for yourself in your lodge,' she said, the firmness of her words underlined by putting the marmalade and honey on to the table with more force than was needed.

As they ate breakfast, the conversation was light and although he often used her name, Libby was mortified that she did not know his, also, it had reached a point when she couldn't ask him! Mentally she went through the list of names. Steve Brilley, writer . . . Mel Edwards, artist, Thomas Davies, composer. Seeming absorbed in plastering his toast with butter and honey, she risked looking at him closely.

As though aware of her scrutiny, he glanced up quickly. 'You can't quite work out which of your four charges I am, can you?'

'You're not Jake Vaunt, he's here already.'

'Jake Vaunt, here? Now that is an interesting surprise.'

'You know him?'

She sounded offhand as though making a casual remark, but her visitor was a keen observer of people.

'Normal curiosity, or have you fallen for him already?'

'Neither!' she replied shortly, getting up to begin clearing the table. 'I know nothing about any of you.'

'I'm mortally wounded that you haven't guessed who I am!'

As she coloured with embarrassment, she saw him smile.

'But then that's why I'm here, a complete change of identity. Don't look so worried, I'm not a prisoner on the run,' he ended suddenly. 'I'll be off, I know my way. Come and see me when you've worked out which one I am.'

CHAPTER TWO

As the remaining two men arrived and introduced themselves, Libby was able to work out that her breakfast visitor had been Steve Brilley, and from the list she had been given, he was a writer. Mel Edwards, the portrait painter, and Thomas Davies, a composer, had arrived mid-morning, the latter's old car making such a noise that she had run to investigate.

'Sorry for the noise,' he apologised, patting the car sadly. 'She is on her last legs, or should that be wheels?'

He looked so vulnerable that she hurried to reassure him and also to introduce herself.

'I'm Thomas Davies,' he said in a way which was almost another apology.

She remembered the words, struggling composer, had been by his name and he certainly looked the part, long-haired, gaunt, thin. She would have to keep an eye on him, see he ate properly.

It was the loud slamming of a car door, which had Libby looking over her shoulder to the other arrival who had parked away from the other vehicles. His whole stance told her that he expected immediate attention and ruffled by this, she turned back to Thomas, pointing out the path to Keeper's Lodge, adding she would follow as quickly as possible.

She didn't hurry to the other man who was now opening and slamming car doors like a petulant child who felt ignored. She glimpsed enough of his face to remember seeing his photograph splashed over the front pages of tabloid newspapers. Hadn't he been caught up in a much-publicised affair with a model? Then a name from her list linked with his face—Mel Edwards, the artist!

Seeing her frown, Mel put down the easel he was taking out of his hatchback. 'If you breathe a word to anyone that I'm here . . .'

'Who you are is no concern of mine,' she replied, hoping she wasn't showing her inward annoyance.

Grant had often said her emotions were so obvious that a blind man would know what she was thinking, feeling!

'My job is to see the smooth running here.' But then she couldn't resist adding, 'But I can't speak for the others.'

'If they've come to this place, they'll want privacy, too, so they're not likely to talk.'

'If you're so worried, I'm surprised you haven't locked yourself away in some luxury apartment,' she said, recalling a little of his frenetic lifestyle.

'Ah, that's what they expect me to do! No-one will think of looking for me in this place!'

Waving a disparaging hand at the carpark, he glanced at her, his slight smile making it obvious that no-one in a million years would think he would willingly associate with someone so unglamorous.

By lunchtime, all three new arrivals were settled in their lodges. Libby felt able to sit down and send a brief e-mail to Mary. Looking again at the list of names, she realised there was no occupation by Jake's. Although she told herself it really didn't matter, nevertheless her curiosity was aroused. She had no idea why the four men needed to come to Sanctuary Wood and if Mary knew, she hadn't passed on the information.

As far as she was concerned, they needed solitude and so did she. Grant had wooed her with a rapid urgency which she had found flattering, rushing into her marriage, much to her family's disapproval. Although they hadn't said so, it was obvious they could not understand why a man like him should fall for an ordinary girl like her.

'Found out who I am then?'

Startled by the voice behind her, Libby turned and, seeing who it was, she was annoyed that he had come quietly and unasked into her private rooms.

'Steve Brilley.' She replied shortly, standing up, and seeing she was taller than him gave her confidence a little boost to be able to look down at him as she said, 'This side of Keeper's Lodge is strictly private. You were sent a plan of it along with the rest of the details so if you look at it, you will see which rooms are for general use.'

'What has happened to an attractive, young girl like you to make you so stand-offish?'

'It's not me who's stand-offish, it's you who's . . . who's . . .'

'Having trouble?'

Momentarily, Libby closed her eyes. Yet another man coming in where he should not! But then realising it was Jake standing behind Steve, she half smiled. 'He's just going.'

Turning, Steve sighed in mock sadness. 'It looks, Jake, as though we're being thrown out.'

'I'm sure you've work to do, if you can call it that,' Jake replied evenly. 'I need to ask Libby something.'

As Jake escorted Steve to the veranda, Libby went into the kitchen. If Jake wanted her for some reason, then she would set firm boundaries for him, too. For a big man, he was very light on his feet, so she hadn't realised he had followed her until he spoke. 'I only came into your room because I heard Steve's voice and guessed he was bothering you.'

She turned quickly and to prevent her colliding with him, he took hold of her arms.

'Sorry,' she gushed out. 'I didn't know you were there.'

Releasing her slowly, gently, he saw her relief. 'You've been hurt.'

The words were so softly spoken she wondered if she had heard correctly. But then briskly he asked if any mail had come for him. Glad of business matters, Libby moved away as she explained that to ensure total privacy, all mail was sent to a central address, then forwarded to her for distribution.

'There's a box outside your door where I put milk, post, or anything you might want from the village. The postman comes late morning but I'm sorry, there was nothing for you today.'

'Thanks.'

Turning, he left quickly, barely giving her time to call out. 'Thank you for rescuing me from Steve.'

Fetching a glass, she went to the fridge for a

carton of orange juice, but just as she took the first sip, she stopped. As well as Mel, Steve also seemed to know Jake, and worryingly, between Jake and Steve, there seemed to be hints of an undercurrent. She could only hope that Sanctuary Wood's peace would not be disturbed.

The evening meal was scheduled for seven o'clock and much to Libby's surprise, everyone came promptly, except for Thomas.

'We'll give him a few more minutes,' she said as the others stood slightly awkwardly by the rectangular pine table which was at one end of the large, bright kitchen.

On a small dresser she had placed red and white wine, cider and beer and she wasn't surprised when Mel took charge of filling glasses. Neither was she surprised when they drank what she had guessed they would—Mel, red wine, Jake, beer, and Steve, white wine which he complained wasn't sweet enough.

'How much longer do we have to wait for that so-called musician?' Mel complained. 'I thought it was supposed to be peaceful here but I've heard him messing about on that electronic keyboard all afternoon.'

'Perhaps he's got carried away,' Libby said, looking anxiously out of the window.

Although her swift glance took in everyone, it lingered slightly longer on Mel who just shrugged.

'I'm starving and it smells so good,' Steve

said, obviously trying to ease the situation. 'Libby, do we have to wait for him?'

With a last glance outside, she asked them to sit down, indicating she would take one end of the table. While Libby placed a large chicken casserole on the table with the accompanying vegetables, Mel and Steve chatted about the weather and the cabins. Jake, she noticed, sat silently, arms folded across his well-muscled chest, eyes fixed on the table. She was not the only one to notice this.

'Cheer up, Jake, it might never happen,' Steve said lightly.

'Perhaps it already has!' Mel's tight smile made Libby shiver, his blue eyes as cold as a winter sea.

'Please, help yourselves,' she urged a little too heartily, sighing with relief as they all complied.

Before sitting down, Libby went once again to the window to look for Thomas. It was Jake who quietly bade her sit down and eat. 'If you're worried about our missing musician, I'll look in on him afterwards,' he offered.

'Aiming to be teacher's pet?' Mel asked acidly.

'It's all right,' Libby intervened hastily. 'I'll go. After all, it is my job.'

Before she served herself, Libby put generous helpings to one side for Thomas, intending to take it to him later. Although one of the few rules was that she would not take the evening meal to the men, she felt just this once she would make an exception. Thomas had looked so anxious, fearful even. Could it be that Mel's attitude in the carpark had put him off?

'That's interesting.' Steve smiled as he watched Libby. 'So when I'm in the white-hot heat of writing and forget the time, to eat, bring my laundry . . .'

'Let's not abuse Libby's good nature.'

Jake glanced at the other two, but there wasn't the slightest hint of a smile to soften his words.

'The main reason for us all coming here is for the peace, solitude. Trying to bend reasonable rules might well trigger resentment.'

'I'm not at all like that!' she replied sharply.

'Libby, I didn't mean you,' Jake said hastily. 'I mean that if one of us makes an extra demand and you were too-good natured to refuse, well . . .'

'I was only teasing.' Steve sighed.

'I hope you all like lemon meringue pie,' Libby asked hurriedly.

The three men finished their meal in silence and when she asked who wanted coffee, Jake was the first to refuse, saying she must be tired after her first full day. Muttering their thanks for the meal, Steve and Mel also refused. Going on to the veranda, Libby watched Steve and Mel wander off together down the path, but Jake, without a word of farewell to anyone, strode off into the wood.

Carefully balancing the tray of food, Libby knocked softly on Thomas's door. She had half expected to hear music, but there was silence. Repeating her knocking, she wondered if she should risk calling out. But suppose he was in the middle of some vital composition? A slight movement at a window caught her eye, but when she looked, there wasn't anyone there. Perhaps it had been a reflection of a tree moving.

Undecided what to do, she finally put the tray on the wooden seat by the door. Thomas would be able to reheat the food, that is if he saw it before night brought an inquisitive fox! She was just leaving when he opened the door and quickly picked up the tray.

'Thanks!' he said, retreating inside, but not before Libby had seen his anxious expression.

'Are you all right?' she asked.

He stopped. 'Yes . . . I'm sorry.'

'Sorry for what?'

'I should have come.'

'It doesn't matter. But even if you're very engrossed with your music, you must remember to come for the evening meal. Shall I ask one of the others to give you a knock when they're coming?'

'No!'

His rebuff was so sharp that she shrugged. 'Please, I'm sorry,' he repeated.

'I've said it's all right,' she said a little impatiently.

'It isn't what you think.'

His reply and downcast eyes had her asking softly. 'Thomas, what is it?'

'I don't think I should have come here. But I've used every last penny.'

'Suppose we go inside and I'll reheat the casserole. You might feel better when you've eaten.'

Waiting until he began to eat, Libby started to say she would go, when he pleaded with her to sit down. Realising he was struggling to find the right words, she told him to finish his meal and then if he wanted to, they could talk. But having just eaten a few mouthfuls, his obvious anxiety had him blurting out, 'I didn't think the others would be . . . well, famous. I'm not in their league.'

'There's no competition here. Who exactly the others are makes no difference. But you all have a common bond, wanting solitude.'

'Except for the evening meal,' he rushed out, then bit his lip as though regretting what he said.

Surely he wasn't so much in awe of Jake, Mel and Steve that he couldn't face sharing a meal with them.

'None of them bite, you know.' Head on one side, she smiled at him.

'They've all made it. I haven't. If I don't come up with something really worthwhile soon . . .' He trailed off despondently.

'How do you know the others haven't come here because of some crisis in their lives or careers?'

'Mel's had several successful exhibitions. I'm not sure exactly what type of books Steve Brilley writes, but from his whole attitude, he's . . .'

'Full of himself,' Libby added before she could stop herself. 'Oh, dear, I shouldn't have said that, should I?'

She pretended to look worried, and unexpectedly Thomas smiled. There was someone on his side!

'That's better,' she encouraged. 'You'll soon get used to them. And Jake is so quiet, he'll not bother you.'

'And what's he famous for?'

She opened her mouth to chide him about his obsession with fame, but instead shook her head. She might have gleaned a little about Mel and Steve, but as for Jake, nothing!

CHAPTER THREE

Libby had felt guilty about removing her wedding ring, but if she was going to make a new start without any awkward questions, then it had to be done before she went to Sanctuary Wood. She had to blink back tears as she put the ring in Grant's silver trinket box. She'd had so much hope for the future on their wedding day, but it hadn't taken long for the first doubts to creep in.

There had been the time he had . . . No, she wasn't going to start on that track. A fresh start meant no looking back, but despite her resolve of making a fresh start, she repeatedly went to the box to look at the ring. So she decided to wear it on a fine gold chain around her neck, concealed by her tops.

Dressing on the second day at Sanctuary Wood, she wore a high-necked, lightweight jumper against the chill wind. Pulling on boots over her cords and picking up her fleece, she slipped a notebook and pencil into her pocket. She had to go shopping, for even though Mary had asked Mr Jones to bring the minimum of groceries, he had made it very plain that shopping was women's work!

Libby decided to call first on Mel who was nearest, but as she walked to Spruce Lodge, she wondered if he would be up, for although it was nine o'clock, she knew so little about the four men that she hoped none of them slept late. As the lodge came into sight, she stopped. Not a good start. The curtains were still closed! But full of enthusiasm for this first complete day in her new job, she headed downhill to Rowan Lodge and Steve. He saw her before she saw him and his welcome greeting had her almost running towards him.

She could really begin her work now!

Lounging on the bench by the door, hands behind his head, Steve's shirt was even more garish than his previous one. Did this, she wondered, mean that he liked to be noticed. She had read somewhere that depressed people often hid behind bright clothes, so it would be interesting to try to discover the true Steve lurking behind the awful shirts!

'I'm going shopping,' she said, standing in front of him, pencil poised over notebook. 'Can I get you anything?'

'I don't know. I'm not used to this sort of thing. My housekeeper takes care of everything.'

'Then we'll just have to go through what you're used to eating. A few small packets of cereals were left for you and milk and sugar.'

She paused, waiting for him to indicate by a word or nod that this was his usual breakfast. But he was looking at her intently as though he had never seen her before. A slight knot of worry tightened her mouth, shadowing her eyes.

'We don't know anything about you, do we?' he said, leaning forward to peer up at her. 'So what's brought an attractive young girl like you to this wooded prison?'

Libby froze. Although she had to some extent created a new identity, she had not expected such outright questioning, such a searching look.

'Ah, so you've problems, too!' he said, leaning back, smiling.

'If you must know, I was fed up with my previous job and wanted a complete change.'

'So was the boss pestering you?'

'No! I don't pry into your reasons for coming here so I expect the same consideration. Not,' she added hurriedly, 'that I have anything to hide.'

'Point taken,' he said, standing up. 'I suppose we had better go and inspect the fridge and cupboards, try to work out what I need to keep this miserable body fed!'

It had taken Libby longer than she had anticipated to complete Steve's list, for although he said he didn't care what he ate, she felt this was a pose and that in reality he liked life to move along without any hiccups.

She did not take the longer, direct path to Birch Lodge, to Thomas, but threaded her way through the trees. Taking care not to tread on the fragile white wood anemones, she was delighted to see bluebells in bud.

Thomas's door was wide open, Libby did not hesitate, walking straight in with a soft, 'Hello?'

Although there was no response, she saw the bedroom door was shut. This was worse than she thought. He hadn't even got up! 'Thomas,' she said quietly, her face close to the wood of the door. 'It's me, Libby. Are you all right?'

27

'Go away!'

'Are you decent?' she asked and, receiving no reply, took a deep breath before opening the door just sufficiently to peer around it.

A hump under the duvet had her standing, hands on hips, as she had seen Matron do when dealing with difficult schoolboys.

'Thomas, hiding away isn't going to achieve anything. Now, I'm going into the kitchen to put on coffee and toast whilst you dress.' She paused and when he still didn't answer she said sharply, 'Thomas, get up! I've not got all day to nanny you!'

Shutting the door noisily, she clattered about in the small kitchen, hoping the smell of coffee and toast would tempt him out and it did. He stood by the little unit separating the kitchen from the living-room, head down, but whether from misery or embarrassment, she couldn't tell.

'Milk? Sugar?' she asked, pouring coffee into two flowered mugs.

Libby liked honey in hot drinks but Mr Jones's shopping list had been kept to basic necessities. She held the mug out to Thomas so he had no option but to take it.

'Drink it, then you'll feel better. Look, Thomas, I've already gone beyond my job description with you, so I'm not going to butter your toast.'

Taking her coffee, she went outside and sat on the bench. If she left him alone, he might pull himself together, but, oh, how she hated that phrase. Grant used to hurl it at her when she dared to say she didn't like the glitzy parties he revelled in, and couldn't she stay at home?

'Libby, I'm sorry.'

Thomas sat down heavily beside her, nibbling miserably at his piece of toast. She sighed, a mixture of exasperation and worry.

Then gently she said, 'Thomas, you said yourself that coming to Sanctuary Wood had been financially difficult. So are you going to let that money go to waste just because the few men here are better known than you? Have you thought that some of them are old enough to be your father? When they were your age, they were most probably struggling too.'

'Jake isn't old enough,'

'Oh, for goodness' sake, don't be so . . . so . . .' She just stopped herself saying childish. That would have achieved nothing. 'I'm younger than you!' she finished lamely.

When he turned to her, puzzled, she added, 'Don't ask me why I said that. It's a useless bit of information!'

'No, it isn't!'

The firmness of his reply startled her, but she kept quiet. Now she had got a positive response from him, perhaps he would say more.

'If you don't mind me asking, what did you do before this?' he asked waving his hand to encompass the trees.

'No, I don't mind. I was a secretary at a boys' boarding school.'

'So this is a complete change.'

'Yes, and that's what I needed, a complete change, a challenge.'

'A challenge!' It was as though Thomas had suddenly woken up and, hitting his thigh with the palm of his hand as though to encourage himself, he added, 'It's a challenge for me, too, isn't it?'

'Yes!' she replied, standing up. 'But a more immediate challenge is to see what shopping you need, so come on, let's make a list.'

Libby then decided to call again on Mel, for surely he would be up by now. But when she saw his curtains were still closed, she was annoyed. It had taken her far longer than she had anticipated sorting out Steve and Thomas, and there was still Jake. At this rate she would be lucky to reach the village by lunchtime!

Going up to Mel's door, she was just on the point of knocking when a quiet voice just behind her warned against doing so. Recognising Jake's deep tone, as she turned, she accused, 'You're always creeping up on me.'

'Sorry! But Mel is an owl, not a lark and if disturbed he can be fierce. So let's move away before our voices wake him.'

'Fierce is a little at odds with being an owl, isn't it?'

'They're deadly hunters,' he said with some feeling. 'But I meant that our dear artist likes to sleep much of the day and party all night.'

'Then he's come to the wrong place!'

'My goodness, you are going to be firm with us! But seriously, from what I've heard, Mel has come here to lick his professional wounds.'

Then seeing Libby's notebook, he guessed the reason for her call on Mel and presuming he would be next, he took a neatly-written, shortlist from the back pocket of his jeans.

'I don't need much shopping. I'm used to surviving on one meal a day and if last night and your excellent cooking was anything to go by, that will be more than enough for me. And as for Mel, buy what you think is best.' Then seeing her frown as she glanced at Spruce Lodge, he added, 'Libby, I know both Mel and Steve and how they can wind people around their little fingers, so I suggest you start as you mean to go on.'

There was something in Jake's voice which brought a kaleidoscope of scenes flashing through her mind. Grant had always told her what to do, how to behave. But Jake appeared not to have picked up her annoyance for he continued.

'And that goes for Thomas, too. Although I don't know him, he looks like a little, lost boy and if you're not careful, he, too, will have you running around after him.'

Snatching his list from him, she shoved it

into the notebook with shaking hands. 'Are you doing this job or me? You might know these people, move in circles with which I'm not familiar, but that doesn't make me a fool.'

'I never said you were,' Jake began, but Libby was already hurrying away.

'Well done!'

A mocking slow handclap from Mel had Jake hurrying away, too.

'Taken a fancy to her, have you?' Mel called after him. 'I think I might try to get her to sit for me!'

If Mary had thought Libby had been driving too fast the day she drove to the unveiling, then she would have been aghast at the speed she now took the narrow lanes to the village. Libby was in the grip of so many emotions, all of them filling her mind with disjointed thoughts—her anger for the way Jake had spoken to her was an echo of what she had felt when Grant had treated her like a child, and she was disappointed. She had come to Sanctuary Wood to make a fresh start but in reality was her life just going on as before? Another man taking Grant's place . . . But she had been married to Grant, taken her vows seriously. Jake was just . . .

The loud blare of a horn jerked her back to the here and now, just in time to swing on the steering wheel to avoid a lumbering lorry. What had she been thinking of, risking her life and that of someone else? Driving like that had been stupid. She had overreacted. Jake was not Grant. But all the same she would have to be on her guard with him.

CHAPTER FOUR

Priorbury still had a lazy feel to it, perhaps because it seemed to have changed little over the years. The stone-built cottages and houses stood sturdily on either side of the narrow main street.

The narrow streets were busy with parked vehicles, and after several attempts, Libby had no success in finding a parking place. Surely there had to be a small carpark somewhere. When she was forced to stop by a lorry unloading, she took the opportunity to wind down a window and ask an elderly man getting into his van. As he turned to reply, she thought she recognised him. Was it the man who had spoken to her on the hill when she had first arrived?

'Yes, Miss Weston, we've a carpark,' he replied. 'Behind the supermarket.'

'I'm sorry, you seem to know me but I don't know you, do I?'

'Mr Jones.' A work-worn, grimy hand reached out towards her. 'Sorry I'm not cleaner, but I've been working since five, not like that lot you've got up there.'

His tone implied very clearly that he had no time for men who didn't do an honest day's hard work. Feeling she had to defend the men at Sanctuary Wood, but not knowing quite what to say, she mumbled something about their work was most probably hard, in its way.

'My Daisy works at the supermarket,' he said proudly. 'Been there since it opened. She'll see you're all right. I was on my way up to the wood,' he continued, 'but I don't think I'll go now with you not being there.'

'Why not?' Libby asked.

Apart from any odd maintenance jobs to do with the lodges, his work with the trees was not her responsibility.

'Do you need to get into Keeper's Lodge for some reason? If so, I'll give you my keys.'

'I don't want to be meddled with.'

'Meddled with? By whom?' Then as it dawned on her that he meant the four men, she said, 'I'm sure you'll be left alone. I'm the one the men come to with problems. Anyway, I won't be long.'

But the only response she got was a muttered comment that they had better not try anything, and he was only going so as not to let her down.

Libby followed Mr Jones' directions to the supermarket which had been built on the site of the old cattle market.

Going in, she stood for a minute to get her

34

bearings and was just setting off towards the breakfast cereals when a plump assistant came hurrying up.

'I've been looking out for you. You'll be needing help.'

'Mrs Jones,' Libby guessed. 'How kind of you. But I don't want to take you away from your work.'

'If you and me is to get on, then I'm not Mrs Jones. I'm not pompous like him,' she said, jerking her head in the general direction of Sanctuary Wood. 'Daisy, that's me.'

Although Libby wanted to look around by herself, she was grateful for Daisy's knowledge of exactly where everything was, the bargains and special offers, and as they went around, Daisy introduced her to the other shoppers, sometimes with a loud, whispered personal comment about them. No-one seemed to mind and in an odd way it made Libby feel welcome, part of the community.

Libby had just begun to sort through the shopping when she got home, when there was a knock on the door. She smiled. Someone was eager for their groceries. It was Jake.

'I thought I'd take my shopping, save you lugging it up the hill,' he said, hands thrust into the pockets of jeans which looked comfortably worn.

'I haven't sorted it out yet,' she flustered. 'But is there anything you want right now?'

'No, but if it's OK with you, I'll sit on the

35

bench outside and wait. Don't hurry. I've all the time in the world.'

As he sat down, legs outstretched, he looked like a man at leisure, but there was a tautness about his face, a slight stiffness in his legs. Going back into the kitchen, Libby tried to recall his exact tone when he'd said he had all the time in the world. Was there an underlying bitterness?

Surrounded by several carrier bags, haste made her clumsy and she dropped a tin of tomato soup on the tiled floor. Picking it up, she grimaced at a dent. Whom had she bought it for? If it was Thomas, he wouldn't notice, but Mel might and complain!

'Look, why don't I help?' Jake said, looking through the open window.

'Thanks, but I can manage,' she replied with more firmness than she was feeling.

'I'm not saying you can't, but many hands make light work and you've spent enough time on us as it is today.'

Again he darkened the doorway, but this time it was fleetingly as he came in.

'Look, let's make a pile on the table for each person. I'll take things out of the carriers and you can place them.'

Libby's protest was cut short by Jake holding up a piece of expensive local cheese.

'Now I guess this isn't for Thomas. Looks more like Steve.'

'It is for Thomas.'

'So our impoverished composer has expensive tastes.' But as Libby put the cheese by Thomas's meagre pile of essentials, Jake added with a smile, 'But perhaps it's a treat.'

The cheese was indeed a treat, but immediately on the defensive, for she didn't want Jake to think she had a favourite, Libby replied. 'Are you going to question me about everything I've bought?'

'I was just making a light-hearted comment.'

'Sorry!' Libby apologised, regretting her sharp reply. 'It's just, well, he seems to be having trouble settling in.'

'When I went by this morning I dropped in, thought I'd be friendly, but he hardly said a word. I felt it would have been better if I hadn't called. He does seem very lost.'

'Aren't we all!'

If Libby could have instantly taken back the words, she would have done. The silence which followed them was as deep as the look Jake was giving her.

'I mean . . .' she stammered.

'That we four men might be here for different reasons, but we've all lost our way somehow?'

'No! I don't know why any of you is here.'

'And what about you, Libby? Do you know why you're here?'

'Well, of course I do! I'm here to run this place.'

'It's a strange job for a young, attractive

girl.'

'That's very sexist of you.'

He groaned, shaking his head in mock dismay. 'Don't tell me it's now wrong to call a girl attractive? If it is, then what's happened to romance?'

'I'm here to work, not to . . . to . . .' Red-faced, she began thrusting some shopping into a carrier bag. 'Here, this is yours,' she said holding it out to him.

Taking it, he reached into his back pocket for his wallet and like an embarrassed young girl, she looked away hastily, as his shirt gaped.

'Pay later, at the month end,' she said. 'Now I've got work to do.'

'Did I detect a slight accusatory emphasis on the "I"? Whatever problems we might have, we're lucky in having Sanctuary Wood as a haven. Many in this world are not so fortunate.'

He was gone before she could ask what he had meant. It was no passing comment, there was something about him, a darkness.

As Libby set out to deliver the shopping to the other three, she could hear the intermittent screech of a chainsaw in the wood, presumably Mr Jones tending trees. Heading towards Spruce Lodge, the sound set her teeth on edge and this had her wondering what the men would have to say about the noise.

Having seen her coming up the path, Mel

was standing at his door, feet apart, hands on hips, face like thunder.

'I was promised peace and quiet,' he shouted over the nerve-jangling noise, as she trudged up the steep path. 'So what are you going to do about it? I can't possibly work in this din.'

'As soon as I've delivered the shopping, I'll find Mr Jones and stop it.'

Reaching him, she held out his shopping, but instead of taking it, he demanded, 'What's this?'

'You weren't up when I called to see what shopping you wanted, so I thought I would get you a few essentials.'

'I came here to avoid setting an alarm clock. I've a good mind to sue for misinformation. This isn't a bit like that so-called brochure of yours.'

'I'm very sorry, but there are bound to be a few teething troubles. I should have asked you all about shopping last night.'

But Mel had no intention of being calmed so quickly. An artist of his repute deserved some consideration, a grovelling apology. Libby's tone had been too matter-of-fact, 'I shall write to Mrs Garfield and complain. We need someone here with experience, not a girl who's little more than a . . .'

'Your shopping!'

Dumping the carrier at his feet, Libby turned, but Mel wasn't about to let her go so quickly.

'So what are you going to do about it?' he demanded.

'Do about what? The fact that you like to lie in bed until all hours?'

Tiredness and the grating chainsaw shortening her temper, Libby knew the impatience in her voice was showing plainly on her face, but she didn't care.

'If you read your brochure, you'll see I'm not responsible for getting you up in the mornings. Now, do you want this shopping or not?'

To her surprise, Mel's attitude changed completely. He was now looking at her with what looked like admiration. But if this was some cunning ploy of his, she was about to be taken in.

Bending to pick up his carrier, she said, 'It doesn't matter to me if you don't want any lunch or breakfast.'

'I'll take it,' he said, snatching it from her. 'And thanks,' he added belatedly as she hurried away, hoping that Steve and Thomas wouldn't be so difficult, but before she saw them, she must try to stop the noise.

Once she was out of sight, Libby stood still, turning her head to try to discover Mr Jones' direction. He seemed to be working higher up, in the steepest part of the wood and with a sigh she began toiling up the hill. It was so muddy in places that she wondered if a hidden

40

spring was seeping through the soil. The higher she went, the worse the path became. A slippery slope now facing her, she paused, wondering whether or not to turn back but then, remembering the men had indeed been promised peace and quiet, she began scrambling upwards, grabbing at protruding tree roots and tufts of grass.

As one clump came up in her hand, she was unable to stop herself sliding backwards. Arms flailing, she tried to keep her balance, but gravity sent her toppling. She hit the ground hard, the force winding her, driving the air from her lungs.

'There, it's all right! Don't panic, it will only make it worse.'

Someone was behind her, kneeling, supporting her lightly, encouraging her. It was only as her breathing eased that she wondered who it was. Because of the chainsaw's noise, she didn't recognise her helper's voice until he said, 'That chainsaw! When I catch up with it I'll . . .'

'Mel,' she said weakly, turning slightly. 'I . . . was going . . . to . . . stop it.'

'Lucky for you, so was I. Let's get you back home.'

Suddenly aware of her position, she tried jerking herself up. She was grateful for Mel's help, but he was much too close. Standing, she swayed a little dizzily and quick to seize the opportunity, Mel put his arm around her again.

'I'm all right, really I am,' she said with growing firmness, but he took no notice. 'Mel, thank you, but I'm fine.'

'You might think so.'

'Leave her alone!'

The harsh command had them jerking apart almost guiltily as Jake came running towards them through the trees.

'It wasn't what you think,' Mel sounded strangely defensive.

'That will be a change for you! But admittedly you do usually go for models and society beauties.'

Leaning against a tree, Libby frowned. What on earth were they going on about?

CHAPTER FIVE

Neither man helped Libby home. Whilst they faced each other, she moved cautiously away. Getting back to Keeper's Lodge seemed to take ages, but as her breathing settled down to its normal rhythm, she began to wonder if she had heard correctly. Replaying what had been said, Jake and Mel seemed to be talking in riddles. When she reached Keeper's Lodge, Steve was just leaving, carrier bags in hand.

Seemingly oblivious of her dishevelled state, he smiled apologetically as he explained that he was hungry and had called for his shopping. Realising she was out and seeing the open door, the carriers on the table, he had taken the liberty of going in and finding his, Wanting him to leave before he noticed her muddy clothes, Libby gave him a little push in the back, urging him to go before he fainted on the spot from hunger! Then, hurrying inside, she shut the door and turned the key.

Refreshed after a shower, she was just brewing a mug of tea and making a cheese and tomato sandwich, when there was a sharp rap on the kitchen window. It was Mr Jones and he was looking far from pleased. 'Who's the boss around here?' he began, as she opened the window.

'Well, in a way I suppose I am,' she said then added hurriedly. 'But, of course, when it comes to the woods, then of course it's you.'

'Then perhaps you'd tell that there man what came ordering me about. Told me if I didn't stop the chainsaw, he'd do it permanently.'

'Oh, dear, I am sorry. How about coming in and having a cup of tea and we'll try to sort something out?'

'Right then, just let me get me boots off.'

Although refusing a sandwich, his hand went repeatedly to the biscuit tin. He seemed calmer now and when she suggested they tried to solve the problem of noise, he seemed quite happy.

'In a way,' she began slowly, 'these men are paying our wages. If they weren't here, I'd be out of a job and I expect you'd only have the tree work to do. The trouble is Sanctuary Wood was advertised as being especially quiet. Perhaps we could sort something out which wouldn't hinder your work but would pacify the others. I really am in a very difficult position.'

'Don't you go fretting. I won't be using the chainsaw for a while. It weren't my intention to get you into bother, but men like them, lazing about, well, I've no time for 'em.'

A spark of mischief had Libby leaning forward and lowering her voice she confided, 'They're not lazing. They are working but it's sort of . . .' She clamped her mouth shut as though she would like to have told him more, but dare not.

'They're all from London, aren't they?' he nodded wisely. 'Enough said. I won't tell a soul about them. You can't be too careful these days. The newspaper and telly people are into everything. You can count on me!'

That afternoon, Libby had a lot of small, time-consuming jobs to do, keeping account of the money she had spent for each man, washing her muddy clothes, e-mailing Mary with the brief daily report and writing to her parents. Although Mary was much older than Libby's parents, they viewed computers and anything to do with them with mistrust. They had not wanted her to marry Grant, but when she had, with such tragic consequences, they had been totally supportive, shielding her from the media who had laid siege to their house when she went back there.

At first they had been delighted when Mary had offered her the job at Sanctuary Wood, but when they discovered she would be the only woman with four men, they had made their feelings very clear to Libby and much to her annoyance, to Mary as well. They seemed to think that having made one unfortunate marriage, Libby needed to be treated like a child.

It took Libby ages to write the short letter for she knew her parents would scrutinise every word, looking for anything which might indicate all was not well. So she kept to generalities, describing Sanctuary Wood, the lodges and what her job involved.

She did not mention the four men by name, saying vaguely they were all famous in their various ways. But as she wrote that, she paused. Certainly this was true of Steve and Mel, and hopefully one day, of Thomas, but what about Jake? What did he do? He had a restless energy which did not go with a normal nine-to-five job. He seemed to know Mel and dislike him. There had been that odd exchange of words about models when Jake had seen Mel helping her after her fall.

For the evening meal, Libby prepared trout

45

and almonds with a green salad. Then thinking that after such a light first course the men, especially Steve, might complain they had not been properly fed, she made a jam roly-poly pudding. She would make the custard at the last moment so there would be no skin or lumps, much disliked by the boys at school!

Surprisingly, Thomas was the first to arrive, and thanking Libby for getting his shopping, he held out the cheese. 'I think this must be for someone else.'

'No, it's yours,' she said, gathering together the cutlery needed for the table. 'You said you liked cheese so I thought you might like to try that local one.'

She had known when she bought the cheese on impulse for him that he had to watch every penny, so now she added, 'I hope you don't mind, but when I brought your shopping, I was going to ask if you would be willing to try it out for me, but you sounded very busy. I thought instead of a pudding one night, I'd try cheese and biscuits, but didn't want to buy a large amount in case it wasn't very good.'

Nodding in agreement, he smiled and she realised it was the first time he had done so, and what a difference it made!

'Look, would you mind laying the table for me? The others will be here soon and the jam roly-poly took longer to make than I had anticipated.'

'This used to be my job at home,' he said,

setting each place.

'Do you come from a large family?' Libby asked.

'No, there's just me.'

In response to the wistfulness in his voice, she confided that she, too, was an only child.

'It's hard, isn't it, being the only one?' he said.

Deliberately, Libby concentrated on cubing cucumber. 'You mean that as we're all they've got, they concentrate too much on us? Wrap us up in cotton wool?'

'So didn't they want you to come here either?' he asked, fetching water and wine glasses from the china cupboard.

'Mine didn't think I would be safe with you lot,' Libby said lightly. 'But what about you? I expect they're proud of your musical ability.'

'My father says music isn't a proper job. He hoped going to music college would get it out of my system, but when I told them I wanted to be a composer, anyone would think I'd said I'd wanted to be the first man on Mars!'

'So what have you done between leaving college and coming here?'

'I play the flute and clarinet and so was able to get a variety of work, enough to save to come here, to really concentrate on composing. I . . .'

But Mel's loud greeting as he came in stopped any further conversation and when he made an acid comment about Thomas helping

Libby, trying to be teacher's pet, Thomas once again resumed a nervous silence. Then crossing to Libby, Mel put an arm around her shoulder. 'Recovered from your little accident? No bruises or bumps, nothing for me to kiss better?'

Shaking herself free, Libby retorted icily, 'Mel, please, let me get on. Go and pour yourself a drink.'

'Oh, dear,' he sighed dramatically. 'I must be losing my touch with women.'

Mel was spun away so sharp from her side, that Libby dropped the bowl of salad dressing on the floor. As it smashed, she heard Jake say harshly, 'What will it take to make you realise that not all women find you irresistible?'

'I was only being friendly. You really must stop thinking the worst of me.'

Libby was too busy sweeping up the glass to see the facial expressions of the two men, but Mel's tone was edged with amusement. Jake's order to him to go and sit down was hard.

'Let me help.' Thomas, obviously embarrassed by the scene between Mel and Jake, bent down by Libby.

'Thanks, Thomas. Could you go into the utility room and get me a mop and bucket and some detergent? This oil is slippery, dangerous.'

'If you hadn't played macho man,' Mel drawled to Jake, 'none of this would have happened.'

'If you had kept your hands . . .'

'For goodness' sake, will the two of you shut up!' Libby hadn't meant to shout but it had the desired effect for Mel sat down, whilst Jake offered to make more salad dressing.

'No, just go to the larder and fetch a bottle of mayonnaise,' she said shortly.

When Steve arrived a few minutes later, he was quick to sense the tense atmosphere and one look at Jake and Mel was enough to tell him they had been at loggerheads. But he wasn't interested in what had happened between the two of them. His concern was for Libby. The atmosphere needed lightening.

'I've been thinking,' he said, 'how nice it would be if Thomas played for us one evening.' Although he was smiling, when he glanced at Jake and Mel, his eyes held a warning.

CHAPTER SIX

Although Libby was very tired, she lay in bed wondering what had happened to cause the animosity between Jake and Mel.

But would it help her, if she knew of the problem? After all, she wasn't there to be a peacemaker between people, but to ensure there was peace for them—but weren't the two intertwined? Suddenly feeling weighed down, she threw back the duvet and got up. She went to the front door and opened it.

It was surprisingly warm for May, so putting her fleece over her night shirt, she curled up on the veranda bench, knees up under her chin. The night sky was cloudless, allowing the stars and moon to cast a magical light.

As she hugged herself for comfort, a sixth sense suddenly sent a shiver of alarm down her spine. Hurriedly she swung her legs down but before she could stand up, Jake's deep voice reassured her. 'Libby, it's me, Jake. Are you all right?'

Startled, she shrank back against the wall, fright tightening her voice as she replied that she was fine.

'I'm sorry if I scared you.'

Wildly, she searched the surrounding tree shadows for any sign of him. Why was he hiding? He had no right to be creeping about at this time of night, frightening her.

'What are you doing?' She had intended her question to be a strong demand, but instead it sounded querulous.

'I could ask you the same,' he replied. 'But if you must know, I've been looking for badgers. Mr Jones has pointed out one or two places, but I was unlucky. I'll have to improve my technique. Animals are much better at detecting an intruder than the average human.'

As he came slowly towards her, she wanted

to dash back inside and slam the door, but she felt incapable of any movement.

'Do you always sit outside at night, not properly dressed? Go back inside before you catch a cold.'

Echoes of Grant treating her like a child had her retorting, 'I'll go when I want to!'

'In that case . . .'

She had never known anyone move so swiftly and silently, not even Grant, who delighted in demonstrating how he got out of dangerous situations. Jake draped his leather jacket around her shoulders but, feeling her tense, left his hands on her shoulders.

'Do you want to talk?' he asked gently. 'I really am sorry if this evening's little scene between me and Mel upset you. It's just that . . .'

She had held her breath for so long she felt she would pass out. Grant used to put his coat around her when they were coming from a party. At first she had liked this seemingly small attention, his concern, but then she had realised it was all part of a charade he liked to play—the seemingly attentive boyfriend, then husband, but there were now no bright lights, no people laughing falsely.

Slowly she exhaled. This wasn't Grant, but nevertheless she didn't want to be touched. Shrugging herself away from Jake's hands, she got up and slipped through the doorway. As she began to close the door, she took off his jacket and thrust it at him.

'Look, why don't you put on something that wouldn't shock the neighbours?' he said softly. 'I could do with a cup of hot chocolate and I'm sure you could after sitting in the cold night air.'

'How did you know I had drinking chocolate?' she began.

'When I went for the salad cream I saw it.'

'No! I'm sorry.'

She hadn't meant to slam the door so hard and as she leaned against it, she whispered, 'I'm sorry.'

Jake strode away, tight-lipped, angry with himself.

To her surprise, Libby slept well, perhaps because of the hot chocolate she had made after she had locked the door and closed the curtains. When guilt edged in the thought that she could have made one for Jake, she banished it by thinking resolutely that it wouldn't have been right for him to have come in.

After eating a quick breakfast and relieved she didn't have to see any of the men until evening, she decided that as she was up to date with all that had to be done, she would spend the morning exploring the wood.

Just in case one of the men should come looking for her, Libby pinned a note on the door, *Back at noon.*

It was sunny and warm, so instead of her

fleece, she pulled on a thick sweater her mother had knitted for her. Taking her walking boots outside, she sat on the bench to put them on. She would have to be careful not to go near Oak Lodge, for the last thing she wanted was to meet Jake. Ever since she had woken and remembered the previous night, she had bit her lip at her own foolishness.

Taking a deep breath, she concentrated on the way she was going. She did not want to fall again! It took nearly fifteen minutes to reach the top of the hill and as this was the wood's boundary, she was able to look down into the next valley. Smoke rose from cottages and houses and in the small fields, tractors were busy finishing the ploughing that a wet winter had delayed. Voices and engine sounds reached her intermittently at the fancy of the wind, and this gave her a strange feeling of detachment. She wasn't part of that world below.

Leaning on a fence post, she sighed. This was the first time for months and months that she felt truly alone, not being watched by Grant and then by family, friends and the media.

She had not felt so carefree since . . . since . . .

Mentally she threaded her way back through the last months of her life. Certainly not since Grant's death, and sadly not on her wedding day, for that had been such an ordeal.

When Grant had come on the scene, he had liked attention, seeming to go out of his way to get his picture and hers in the papers. When she hesitantly told him she didn't like it, he had called her his little mouse and said that in his job he had to keep his name in the public eye.

Despite the noise and sometimes cheekiness of the boys at the school, she had been carefree there. Although she was the secretary with no direct responsibility for the boys, she had helped out when needed and had enjoyed it. When flu had stretched Matron and her nurse, Libby had happily helped.

The roar of Jake's motorbike indicated he was leaving Sanctuary Wood and Libby walked back with more ease. Now there was no risk of seeing him until the evening and then the others would be there.

'Hi, there, Libby!' Steve was hurrying towards her, and to her surprise it looked as though he, too, had been walking.

'Been for a walk?' she asked as he caught her up.

'I might not have Jake's athletic build or be as thin as a rake like Thomas, but when I need to, I walk. And believe me, I need to!'

'Need to?' she asked.

Had his doctor told him to take more exercise? He certainly was overweight. Shouldn't she be aware of any health problems?

Putting his hand on her arm, Steve sounded anxious as he asked if she had time to come and have a cup of tea. When she nodded, he linked his arm through hers, walking so fast that she laughingly asked him to slow down. Reaching Rowan Lodge, Steve was in such a hurry to brew the tea that he slopped water from the kettle over the floor. When he clumsily knocked two mugs together, Libby took them from him.

'Steve, calm down!' she soothed. 'Suppose you sit down and tell me all about it whilst I brew the tea?'

She smiled encouragingly as he began one sentence after another, only to stammer to a halt. Carrying the mugs into the sitting area, she gave him his as he paced about. Watching his tea spill over the edge of his mug, she sighed inwardly. Tomorrow she must remember to remove the stains from the carpet!

'Steve, what is it? Would it help to talk?'

'I want to. Meeting you like that, it was fate. Do you believe in fate?' But not waiting for an answer, he rushed on, 'I feel you're sympathetic, wouldn't laugh. But if I tell you, you won't tell the others, will you?'

'Of course not,' she said.

'I write, wrote romances.'

He glared down at her as though to stop any levity on her part. 'That's nice,' she said, at a loss. 'But you said wrote. Have you got writers' block or something? Is that why you've come here?'

'You're not surprised? Don't you find it funny that a man like me writes under the name of . . . No, I'm not telling you that because then you really would laugh and I couldn't bear it!'

'I won't laugh, whatever you tell me,' she promised.

'I've written other novels as well, under another pen name, but it's romances which have put jam on my bread. It's only my agent and publisher who know my true identity. When my last wife found out about the romances, she laughed every time she set eyes on me. Said it was the funniest thing she had ever heard. When I couldn't take her constant jibes any longer, we parted, she taking the house and a large slice of my bank account as the price for her silence.'

'I don't think it's at all funny,' Libby said. 'You write books which people enjoy, don't give them nightmares and I think that's good. There's too much nastiness in the world as it is.'

As a tabloid newspaper picture of Grant lying dead sprang into her mind, she closed her eyes as though to black it out.

'You've suffered some dreadful experience?' he asked gently.

'I'm not here to talk about me,' she said, sitting up straighter in the chair. 'But I'm not sure I can help you with a problem to do with writing. I've no experience.'

'But you read. I've seen the books you brought here. Mysteries!'

He sat down opposite her, eyes now bright with excitement. 'Yes, I've writers' block, for the first time in my life. I'm too scared to even open my laptop in case I can't write a single word.'

'If you let your wife's unkindness affect you like this, then she might laugh even more. You won't want that, would you?' Then as she remembered the excited way he had mentioned her books and that they were mysteries, things fell into place. 'You're thinking of writing a mystery! How exciting! I love them, always have. No bodies though. I don't like murders.'

'There, I knew it was fate that brought me here! Libby, I know it's not part of your job, but can I tell you some of my ideas? See if they sound good?'

'Of course you can. It would be a privilege.'

CHAPTER SEVEN

Part of the service offered was that residents' mail could be directed to Mary who then sent it on. This way, it was hoped the whereabouts of those in Sanctuary Wood would not be known. The postman always came mid-afternoon and Libby then had to sort out the mail for each lodge and deliver it if she had time, otherwise it could be collected when the men came for their evening meal.

That day, there was nothing for Thomas or Jake and only two for Steve, both looking like bills. Mel's only letter was in a pale pink envelope and as she wafted it under her nose, it still held the very faint scent of . . . was it rose?

She had hoped the hurt of Grant's unfaithfulness would have gone, but it hadn't. Snapshots still occurred of the sly glances from others in his circle, the whispers, the knowing laughs . . .

Hurriedly snatching up the mail, she decided to deliver it. Perhaps seeing Mel and Steve would give her something else to think about, even if they only exchanged a few words. She went to Steve first and as she knocked on the door, she was surprised when he shouted, 'Go away. I'm busy.'

'I've brought your post. I'll leave it in the box.'

'Libby, I don't want an evening meal. I'm working!'

The excitement in his voice banished all thoughts of Grant. Steve must have started on his new book, the mystery! Heading towards Spruce Lodge in a happier state of mind, she scrutinised the pale pink envelope. Who was it from? Certainly a woman and a flamboyant one, for who used scented stationery these days? But as she neared Mel's lodge, a torrent of angry words stopped her. At whom was he shouting?

'I wouldn't disturb him if I were you.'

At the sound of Jake's voice, she turned around in surprise. Where had he sprung from? He always moved very quietly, but why hadn't she heard his bike? Then thinking it looked as though she was standing there deliberately listening, she held up the letter.

'I was going to give him this,' she rushed out.

'I don't think he's in the mood for personal delivery, unless of course you think it's important. Didn't you know Mel took his rôle as a famous artist very seriously, temper tantrums and all?'

'But he's by himself, isn't he?' she puzzled.

With a warning finger to his lips, Jake took the letter and dropped it in the box, closing the lid quietly. Then taking Libby's arm, he led her away so that if Mel stopped raging, he wouldn't hear them.

'Perhaps you haven't wanted to read the newspapers much recently, but Mel's fall from favour has been widely written about. It seems his portraits have been upsetting sitters and also those who paid out huge sums for him to do them. He thinks every woman is fair game for his amorous attentions. I still can't

59

understand it, but even the most level-headed fall for it, thinking they will be the one who will persuade him to be faithful, marry them even.'

Glancing at him, Libby saw the same tension in his face she had noticed before. Could it be that Mel had split up Jake and a girlfriend, his wife even? Is that why he had come to Sanctuary Wood, only to find Mel there, too?

'He's hurt you,' she said quietly.

Jake nodded, then sighed. 'It was some time ago. Rosie was beautiful, a model. Perhaps you saw her pictures in glossy magazines. But take away the make-up and wonderful clothes and she was just normal, fun to be with. You wouldn't have seen her at any of the smart parties you went to, unless she was forced to go for some publicity stunt. Mel saw her at one and, well, the rest, as they say, is history.'

'But surely she didn't dump you for him?'

His silence telling her this had been so, she asked gently, 'Is that why you came here?'

'Good heavens, no!' Turning, he looked at her directly, but although his mouth held a slight smile, the tension was still there in his face, his eyes. 'I'm over it, but when I see him, I can't help remembering the many relationships he's ruined. I'll admit I would rather he wasn't here but his presence is a minor irritation compared with . . .'

As Jake pressed his tips tight as though

afraid to say any more, Libby realised he knew who she was.

'Please don't say anything to the others,' she whispered.

It might have been that she was meaning about Mel, but they both knew this wasn't so.

'We've all come here with secrets of one sort or another,' he said, touching her face lightly. 'And secrets they should remain, unless the owner wants, needs, to share them.'

Later, just as Libby was thinking about the evening meal, Mel phoned her briefly to say he would not be coming. She wasn't sorry, as he still sounded angry. So that left just Thomas and Jake . . .

Mr Jones had arrived late that morning, muttering that his van had broken down, and after checking with Libby there weren't any maintenance problems, he had left to inspect boundary fences, a job he assured her would be quiet. Although she had told him there was no need for him to call in when he was leaving, he insisted it was only proper she should know, adding that after that, if there was any noise in the wood, he couldn't be blamed.

True to his word, he came to say he was going, and to her surprise, she saw Jake was with him and Mr Jones was actually smiling!

'I'm off now,' he said. 'I'm giving Jake a lift to get his bike back from the garage. He was going to walk to the village. It seems at least one of 'em isn't frightened to put one foot in front of the other. But I told him the sooner he gets there, the sooner he can get back.' Then turning to look up at the sky, he added, 'I give it just thirty minutes before it rains as though someone up there has left the tap running. You watch, I'm never wrong.'

Libby watched, astonished, as the two men walked companionably side by side, Mr Jones pausing to point out something of interest in the trees. What could have happened to change Mr Jones' opinion towards at least one of the men, Jake?

As predicted, the sky darkened and the heavens opened just at the time Mr Jones had said and above the noise of the running gutters, Libby heard the returning roar of Jake's motorbike. Would his leathers have kept him dry? Should she . . . But shaking her head slightly in reproach, she warned herself not to get too involved with him. She turned her thoughts to Thomas. He seemed incapable of taking care of himself. If he got a wetting coming for the evening meal, he was so thin and pale he would surely go down with a chill!

Going to the phone, she punched in his number. 'Thomas, have you got waterproofs?' she asked. 'Good, I'm glad your granny gave you her large umbrella when she knew you were coming here.'

Replacing the handset, Libby smiled. What an odd present to give someone, but it was certainly useful.

As she turned to go into the kitchen, a tall, dark shape standing just inside the doorway, made her gasp with fright. Jake!

'Sorry if I frightened you,' he apologised, moving into the light shining from the table lamp she had switched on. 'I can't seem to get out of the habit of moving quietly. Perhaps I should sew bells on my clothes! Libby, I've come to apologise. I shouldn't have unburdened myself on you like that. You have enough to contend with as it is.'

Then, bringing one hand from behind his back, he held out a bunch of bedraggled lilies. 'I'm sorry, they were the last ones in the shop and being in the bike pannier hasn't helped either.'

'Thank you. I'll find a vase.'

Taking them, she wondered if she had heard the slight tightness in her voice. No-one had given her flowers since Grant, and then his had been opulent bouquets delivered by a florist when he knew he had upset her. Grant never said sorry, but he always wanted her to apologise all the time. It was never his fault if they were late anywhere, it was hers, whatever the true reason.

'Am I forgiven?'

'What? Oh, sorry. I was miles away,' she said hastily, looking around the sitting-room for a vase although she knew there wasn't one there.

'Those miles looked as though they were

going to a place with sad memories,' Jake said softly. Then more briskly he added, 'It looks as though Mary has slipped up in her furnishing of this place. No vases.'

'She wouldn't want to encourage the picking of wild flowers, especially as some of them are protected by law, and anyway, I doubt anyone would send me flowers. My family isn't like that.'

Although she had said the last sentence with a half laugh, to her surprise Jake looked grim, but it was so fleeting she thought it might have been a trick of the light.

'Perhaps there might be something suitable in the kitchen,' he suggested, standing aside to let her pass.

As Libby began opening cupboards, it seemed quite natural for him to do so, too, and it was he who brought out a pottery water jug.

'I usually put that on the table. Thomas seems to like water.'

'Well, just for tonight, he can go to the tap. I doubt these poor things will last until tomorrow, and talking about tonight, I hope I haven't hindered you.'

Filling the jug with water and gently arranging the flowers, she shook her head. 'There'll only be you and Thomas.'

'Perhaps the pink envelope contained unpleasant news. Perhaps this time the lady isn't for dumping,' he said with a smile as he misquoted Margaret Thatcher.

'Mel was shouting at himself before he could have seen the letter. Perhaps his work isn't going very well. To be honest,' she confessed, turning to face him, 'I've never heard of Mel, but I guess I'd better not tell him that!'

'Look, Libby, you could say it's none of my business, but only see him when you have to. He could make an old hag feel beautiful, that she was the only one in the world for him.'

'Are you calling me an old hag?' she accused lightly.

'No! And to prove it . . .'

His tender kiss was so fleeting that she didn't have time to react. Or had she? Had she, she wondered, returned it?

'I shouldn't have done that either,' he sighed. 'I'm making quite a fool of myself today, aren't I?'

But as she whispered, 'No, you're not!' he went towards the door as though he hadn't heard.

'Don't go! It's pouring down still. And anyway, you'll soon have to come back.'

'Thanks. I promise not to misbehave.'

'You haven't as far as I'm concerned.'

She had meant to say that it didn't matter, but to her horror it sounded as though she welcomed kisses from men she hardly knew. What must he think of her? But then it was he who had kissed her.

'Libby, you're standing there as though

you've all the worries of the world on your shoulders. Are you sure you want me to stay?'

Trying to sound casual, light-hearted, she said, 'I wouldn't let a dog out in that rain! Perhaps you would like to take off your jacket. It can get hot in here.'

Momentarily she closed her eyes. Why had she said that? Thankfully, Jake had gone into the small hall where he hung up his jacket and took off his boots.

When he returned, he paused in the doorway to strike a pose as though for a fashion magazine.

'What the well dressed man wears for dinner with a charming girl!' Lifting up his right foot, she saw his big toe sticking through a hole in his sock.

'Would it be better if I took off my socks?' he asked. 'Which do you think will embarrass Thomas more, seeing my big toe, or all of them?'

Although pretending to be deep in thought, she was experiencing a lightness of heart that she hadn't felt since she had become deeply involved with Grant.

'Leave your sock on for then he will see you as just a normal human being, not superman.'

'It's a shame he's so nervous of us all. Well, not quite all, for he seems to be relaxed with you.'

'I'm not anyone famous, am I? Though, come to think of it, I've another confession to make. Jake, showing my ignorance again, I'm sorry, but I don't know what you do.'

Libby's apologetic smile faded as, pointedly ignoring her question, he went towards the utility room.

'I guess you prepare vegetables in here,' he said. 'Shall I peel potatoes?'

Stunned by his change of mood and also that she had so clumsily brought this about, she avoided looking at him as she muttered that as there were just the three of them, she thought they would have a simple meal of jacket potatoes, grilled ham, eggs and tomatoes.

'The potatoes will need scrubbing,' he said, but just as he opened the door to the utility room, she exclaimed, 'Now it's me who should be apologising!'

'Perhaps we've both done enough of that for one day,' he replied. 'Let's pretend today never happened.'

'Fine by me.'

She smiled, but she knew she wouldn't be able to erase the memory of his kiss.

CHAPTER EIGHT

As if by mutual agreement, as soon as Thomas arrived, Jake and Libby acted as though nothing had happened. But when Thomas saw

Jake was in his socks, he seemed embarrassed.

Taking the jacket potatoes from the oven, Libby suddenly had a startling thought which nearly made her drop them. Surely Thomas had not thought that Jake being shoeless meant there was something going on between them. What could she say that would make it clear what had happened, without it seeming too pointed?

Whether or not Jake had also felt Thomas's embarrassment she couldn't tell, but he began teasing Thomas gently, and to Libby's astonishment the normally shy musician seemed to enjoy it, even at times setting himself up. As Thomas seldom had the courage to look at people directly, he didn't seem to notice Libby and Jake weren't quite able to look each other in the eye either. Under Jake's skilful questions, Thomas told them about his musical ambitions, delighted that here were two people whom he greatly admired, showing an interest in him and what he hoped to achieve.

When the meal ended however, instead of sitting around the table chatting over several cups of coffee, Thomas seemed so eager to leave that he almost ran out of the door.

'Have I put my foot in it again?' Libby asked.

She hoped Jake would make some comment which would show her previous questioning of him had been forgotten and forgiven, but he was already pulling on his boots, and, gathering up his helmet and leather jacket, he left with just a brief thanks for the meal.

It had stopped raining and, standing in the doorway, she called out her thanks for the flowers, but he appeared not to have heard for he was soon lost in the deep shadows of the wood.

Most of the washing-up she stacked in the dishwasher, the rest she left for morning. Libby then curled up on the sofa in the living-room, and although she had opened the mystery book she was reading, her eyes kept drifting to Jake's lilies. They had revived in water and she thought how nice they looked and there was a faint perfume, too. If only she hadn't spoiled things by questioning Jake! That was the very thing Mary impressed on her she must not do, question. What also added to Libby's guilt was the fact that she herself had taken the job at Sanctuary Wood to get away from questioning!

Restlessly throwing down the book, she decided to go for a walk. Exercise and fresh air would take her mind off Jake, her stupidity, and also might help her to sleep. But she wasn't the only one needing fresh air, for Mel, too, was out and, recognising Libby's slight silhouette in the twilight, he called out to her softly, 'Libby, sorry I missed the meal but things aren't going as planned.' Then as he caught up with her, he asked with unusual

69

courtesy, 'Can I join you? Or are you frightened your reputation will be damaged beyond repair?'

'I'm sure your behaviour would have a saint applauding,' she replied lightly, and although she would have preferred to be alone, she moved slightly to one side, indicating he could join her.

In silence, they walked downhill for several minutes, sometimes dodging to one side as a tree shed the last of its burden of rain. The path became more overgrown, narrowing, and as Mel led the way, he held back sprays of the new growth of wild roses and brambles.

He seemed so intent on doing this that when he suddenly asked, 'Do you know why Jake hates me?' Libby was taken by surprise.

'Pardon?'

'Mary didn't tell you then?'

Although he had stopped, turning to face her, the fading light prevented him seeing her expression.

'No, she only briefly told me your individual expertise.'

'Did she tell you about Jake?'

Was he going to tell her the reason for Jake being at Sanctuary Wood? If so, she didn't want to know. If there was a secret to be brought out in the open, then it was up to Jake. Trying to divert Mel, she asked if he knew Mary well.

'Sort of,' was the vague reply. 'She's very

much tuned in to anything of an artistic nature and we'd had a good discussion at my last exhibition. I seem to remember she bought a small picture of a child.'

Relieved to have distracted him, Libby suggested they turn back as it was getting late, but Mel wasn't to be so easily diverted from his objective. Taking her arm, he repeated his first question. Annoyed at the way he was holding her and by his insistence, she replied shortly that she knew nothing about any of them, whether they had known one another before they came to Sanctuary Wood, and anyway, wasn't interested.

Breaking free from his grasp, she began walking quickly up the path, until he called after her. 'He thinks I stole his girlfriend!'

'I know,' she replied shortly.

Then annoyance had her asking, 'If you're so eager to tell me why you think Jake is here, what's your reason for being here?'

She thought he would stride off in anger, but instead he caught up with her. 'No-one seems to want my portraits any more. I want my sitters to look beautiful, but these days painters show the character of the sitter, whatever that is.'

'Perhaps it's what makes them who they are,' Libby suggested.

Then feeling suddenly very tired, she continued up towards Keeper's Lodge. She knew he was following and assuming that, like her, he didn't want to continue their conversation, she was surprised when he said in despair, 'I just don't know what to do now. Any ideas?'

She sighed. 'If you like, we'll talk tomorrow.'

'I would rather now. I don't want the others to know.'

'I certainly wouldn't tell them!'

When he replied that things had a nasty habit of getting out, she wondered if he was thinking about his affairs with sitters.

Later, looking back, she couldn't remember inviting him in, or making a cup of tea, nor could she recall the often disjointed path of their conversation. But somehow they had arrived at the seemingly odd idea that he should try painting landscapes. Whatever, he had left happy, thanking her profusely for her help. But despite Mel's eagerness that no-one should know he had been talking to Libby, someone else did . . .

Although all the lodges were equipped with a vacuum cleaner, cloths for mopping up spillages, and dusters, it was part of Libby's duties to clean them properly once a week.

So, the following morning, having heard the faint sound of Thomas's keyboard, she went there first. Although he seemed to have been hard at work, he was pleased to see her and got in her way by trying to help her.

'Thomas,' she said after the two of them

had done a little dance trying to get out of each other's way, 'Look, if you leave me to it, I'll be finished much sooner.' But then seeing his disappointment, she added hurriedly, 'But I really would like it if you played to me whilst I work. Perhaps one of your own pieces?'

Smiling broadly he began playing quietly. Libby had been expecting modem music which to her seemed full of discord, but to her surprise, his music was gentle, romantic, so much so that a few times she found she had stopped work to listen. Putting away the cleaning things, her thanks were genuine. 'Thomas, thank you, that was lovely. I enjoyed every minute of it.'

'Everyone says that, except the people who matter,' he said wryly. 'I came here to try to write something more . . . more . . . Oh, I don't know!' he said, crashing out a painful discordant.

'I know it sounds a daft thing to say, but perhaps you're trying too hard,' she suggested softly. 'I have to admit I know nothing about music, but suppose you thought about something you enjoy, and see if it inspires you.' Although he smiled his thanks, he sat, head bowed, hands idle.

'Aren't boys supposed to like trains and football?' she asked brightly.

'I didn't.'

'Well, apart from music, what else did you do?'

'Computer games.'

'There you are then!' she exclaimed. 'How about thinking of your favourite game and letting your imagination come up with pictures which you can turn into music?'

As she left Birch Lodge, she heard a few hesitant notes and smiled. Hopefully, Steve too, would have made a good start of his mystery novel! But as she knocked tentatively on his door, he came to the window, a hand waving the would-be caller away. Then seeing it was Libby, he smiled and hurried to open the door wide.

'Libby, sorry, I didn't mean for you to go away. Please, come in.'

Her heart sank as she saw the mess. Steve obviously didn't believe in putting anything away or washing up the few mugs and plates, but she was glad to see from the scattered papers by the laptop that he appeared to have been working.

Fetching the vacuum cleaner, she asked, 'How's it going?'

'I think I might have the germ of an idea, but I don't want to discuss it yet.'

Mel, having left a note propped up in the window telling her he would be out all day and to go in, Libby was able to move on to Oak Lodge much sooner than she had anticipated. Although normally the steep path would not have troubled her, as she drew near Jake's, she became slower and slower. Much as she had tried to push aside memories of the previous evening, his kiss, she could recall every minute. But just as Oak Lodge came into sight, she stopped.

She was just about to go away, when Jake called out, 'Not coming? I wonder why.'

His tone was so heavy with sarcasm that she frowned with puzzlement. Surely last night's kiss couldn't be the reason, especially when it was he who had kissed her.

Taking a deep breath to steady her rapidly-pumping heart, she went towards him, but looked down as though having to concentrate on the path.

'After what I said about Mel, you chose to take no notice.'

She stopped on the slope a few steps away from him and so he was able to look down at her, eyes as hard as granite. 'It isn't what you think,' she began.

'Isn't it? If he hasn't added you to his list of conquests, then what was he doing leaving your place last night?'

His accusatory tone and his stance brought an instant picture of Grant which ignited her swift, cutting response. 'Think what you like. I don't have to explain to you what I do.'

Turning abruptly, she headed back towards Keeper's Lodge and although she wanted to run, she resisted the urge. How dare he think she would be silly enough to fall for Mel!

CHAPTER NINE

For the first time since she had arrived, Libby had an overpowering urge to get away from Sanctuary Wood. Stopping just long enough to wash and change into more respectable cords, she ran towards the carpark. Feeling the need for company, however anonymous, she drove into Priorbury.

Going into the curiously named Humming Bird Tea Rooms, she immediately knew why it was so named, for a gentle hum of talk and gossip filled the small room. As she stood looking for a vacant table, several people looked at her, smiling when they caught her eye. Assuming the grey-haired woman in a white, poppy strewn dress, was waving at someone else, Libby looked away, but then frowned as she was addressed by name.

'Miss Weston, it's me, Daisy! There's a seat here.'

Colouring as she became the focus of several pairs of interested eyes and with great reluctance, Libby went to Daisy's table. 'Sorry, I didn't recognise you,' she apologised, pulling out a chair.

'I look different out of that uniform they make us wear. If they'd let me choose it, we would be dressed in nice bright colours. They make you feel better, don't they?' she said, frowning slightly at Libby's navy cords and blue sweater.

Luckily, Libby was saved from answering by the appearance of a bored-looking, gum-chewing young girl who demanded to know if she'd made up her mind yet?

'I've told you before, you keep a civil tongue in your head,' Daisy admonished. 'It's no way to keep folk coming back.'

Hurriedly, Libby scanned the menu, selecting a cheese salad and brown bread.

As the girl slouched away, Daisy leaned across the table. 'I could tell you a thing or two about that family, but I'd better hold my tongue.'

Libby's relief that she was going to be spared gossip was short-lived for Daisy promptly began telling her about other people in the Humming Bird, in a loud whisper.

'Don't let me keep you,' Libby said when Daisy had finished her steak and kidney pie, chips and peas.

'I've not finished yet! What's going on up there then? Some of those men been giving you trouble, have they? You should have told Mr Jones. He would have sorted 'em out for you!'

'There's no trouble.'

'Then why did Mrs Garfield ring to tell Mr Jones to keep an eye on you?'

'What exactly did she say?'

Libby hoped she sounded only faintly

interested.

'He wouldn't tell me. Said it was between her and him, but it must have been important for he puffed out his chest like she'd asked him to do something special.'

'It must be something to do with the trees,' Libby said as she got up, but inwardly she worried.

Mary was not one to go bothering people without a very good reason.

Wanting to catch Mr Jones and find out why Mary had phoned him, Libby hurried back to Sanctuary Wood, anxious to find him. Although his van was still there, he was nowhere to be seen, but he did as usual come to tell her he was going and that's when she asked him bluntly what Mary's call was about.

Realising from whom Libby had obtained the information, Mr Jones muttered, 'She's worse than a town crier!' Then to Libby, 'It's nothing to bother yourself about. Mrs Garfield just wanted to go over a few things with me, about the wood.'

Before she could question him further, he had hurried away. She was just going to phone Mary, when Jake arrived. 'Have you a minute?' he asked.

'If it's about your cleaning, I'll do it tomorrow.'

'No, it isn't, but anyway I'll do it myself.'

'It's my job,' she began defensively.

'I'll not have you doing my cleaning. Mary

should never have asked you to do it. She should have got someone in from the village.'

'Don't be so silly! I'm not afraid to do a bit of housework.'

'I don't think it's suitable.'

'Suitable?' she shrilled. 'Who are you to know what is or isn't suitable for me? You're worse than Grant!'

As soon as she said his name, she wished she could disappear.

'There's no need to look so panic-stricken,' he said softly. 'Being able to say his name is a step back to normality.'

'You knew him?'

'It was inevitable that we sometimes ended up in the same zones of conflict.'

'He never mentioned you.'

'Grant was only matey with people who could be useful and I was just a stills photographer.'

Libby bit her lip, then taking a deep breath rushed out, 'Were you there when . . . ?'

'No! And if I had been, I would never have used my camera. What happened was unforgivable. There's a very fine line between what's acceptable and what isn't. It's no excuse, but if Grant hadn't always wanted to be in the public eye . . . You can work well, have professional recognition, without always being in the newspapers yourself. You had never heard of me and neither have most people, but in my way, I was as good as Grant.'

'I didn't want to be known, recognised. But you've recognised me,' she said miserably.

'We've been to the same award ceremonies, and I've a good memory for faces, especially one like yours.'

Looking at her closely, he seemed to be on the point of adding something but then said softly, 'You were pushed into the limelight. Is that why you came here? To get away from it all, hoping you'll be forgotten?'

'I wanted to get back to being just me. Does that sound silly?'

For the first time, she glanced up at him, but he seemed to be looking through her as though remembering something.

'You, too?' she asked.

'Me, too.' Now he met her eyes and they were so full of pain that she gasped. Then taking hold of her shoulder he said firmly, 'But we'll win through, both of us.'

Libby had not thought it possible for four, seemingly hungry men to eat a meal so quickly and silently, but the atmosphere wasn't unpleasant that evening, for they were all deep in thought. With Steve, Thomas and Mel, hopefully this was to do with their work, but what about Jake? Was he still thinking about what they'd said earlier, the reason why he had come to Sanctuary Wood? He knew why she was there, but she didn't know why he was there!

'When is it laundry day?' Mel broke the

silence.

'I should have asked you to bring it this evening,' Libby flustered. 'I'll come and collect it later.'

I'll do that,' Thomas said. 'I need fresh air. I won't disturb you, Libby. I'll leave it on the veranda.'

Jake was the first to leave and as Libby came to the door with him, he smiled. 'You've an admirer there.'

'Don't be so silly!'

'Why not? Remember, it's time to move on.'

'What about you?' she asked.

She meant him moving on, too, but he replied, 'You mean Thomas and me coming to blows over you?'

'No! I didn't mean that!' she denied.

'Why not? It's all part of life, two men vying for the attention of a beautiful woman.'

He was smiling. Did he really mean it, or more likely, was it a gentle tease?

Next morning, after carrying in the four boxes of laundry and setting the washing machine going for the first load, she phoned through an order to the supermarket. Daisy took the order and she said she would see to it at once and it would be delivered that afternoon. The greengrocer was equally helpful.

Washing machine and tumble dryer both working noisily, Libby didn't hear Mr Jones until he came into the utility room and from his face she knew he wasn't in a good mood. 'I'm nothing but a dogsbody. I've been told to bring your groceries, then as I was loading that, I was asked to bring your veg and things. To cap it all, the postman gave me this lot.'

'You're very kind,' Libby began, taking the packet of mail from him. 'Would you like a coffee before you start?'

'Start? I started at cock crow this morning, long before any of you lot were stirring. And as acting as errand boy has set me back, I've no time for coffee.'

He left, shoulders hunched as though carrying the weight of the world. Going into the kitchen, Libby emptied the packet of mail Mary had sent, along with a note to Libby. After saying how pleased she was to receive Libby's e-mail reports and that all seemed to be going well, Mary asked after Jake, saying that whilst Libby had mentioned the other three, she hadn't mentioned him. Was he, Mary asked, all right?

No, he wasn't, she thought, and Mary's enquiry made her resolve to try to help him.

There wasn't much mail for the men, for coming to Sanctuary Wood to get away from the world, they had only given the forwarding address to people who really mattered. Steve's one envelope had a computer-generated label on the bottom of which was the address of his agent. Good news hopefully. Thomas had two hand-written letters, Libby guessed from family. For Mel, there were three pink envelopes, all addressed in the same flamboyant hand. Libby smiled. Whoever she was, she certainly was persistent! Jake though as usual, had nothing, a sure sign he was cutting himself off completely from the outside world.

But the outside world was just about to invade Jake's privacy. Hearing the powerful engine long before it reached Sanctuary Wood, Libby hurried to the carpark. Someone had most probably taken the wrong turning. The low-slung, bright yellow sports car came so fast towards the gate, that Libby feared it would smash right through, but bringing the car to a stone-scattering halt, the driver leaned out to demand, 'Is this Sanctuary Wood?'

She nodded but made no attempt to open the gate. One of the rules was that visitors contacted Mary and she in turn would ask Libby to check if a visit would be welcome. Having received no such message, Libby guessed this man had come on the off chance of seeing one of the men.

'Open the gate, will you?' It was a demand rather than a request.

'This is private property.'

'I've come on business, not that it's anything to do with you.'

'It has everything to do with me. I'm the manager.'

'Then be a good girl and open that . . .'

'Thank you, Libby. I'll deal with him.' From Jake's slight breathlessness, it was obvious he had come running.

'Jake . . .' she began.

'I said, go!'

When he underlined his order by pointing back towards Keeper's Lodge, his visitor clapped softly.

'That's what I was hoping for. A return of your fighting spirit.'

Having got out of the car, the man came towards the gate and even if she hadn't liked his manner before, his arrogant swagger and hardness of face annoyed Libby instantly. 'Jake, if you don't want to see him . . .'

'Libby, please, go!' Taking her by the shoulders, Jake pushed her. 'I want you away from here.'

More of an entreaty than an order, Libby obeyed, but reluctantly.

As Jake and the man were now confronting each other over the gate, she went just far enough into the wood so she could not be seen.

'Karl, how did you find me?' Jake demanded harshly.

'Oh, come on, you of all people should know you can't just disappear in this country. It takes a lot of expertise and effort to vanish without a trace. Now, are we going to your hut or shall we go somewhere more civilised? Roughing it might be normal to you, but I prefer to talk in comfort.'

'I told you before, there is nothing to talk about.'

Libby's heart was beating so rapidly with alarm that she put her hand over it as though this would magically ease it.

'Libby, it's me,' a voice spoke quietly behind her.

Turning, she was so relieved to see Mr Jones.

'Trouble, is there?' he mouthed.

'An unwelcome visitor for Jake.'

'Right, we'll see about that.'

Moving silently through the trees towards the gate, Mr Jones seemed suddenly to appear by Jake and he was holding a large pruning knife!

'Be careful as you turn your car,' he said in a matter-of-fact way. 'The grass is soft and you wouldn't want to damage your car, would you?'

Although Karl had backed away, holding up his hands as though to ward off an attack, he still had one last try at persuading Jake to talk.

'Come on, stop this silly charade. This is a civilised country.'

'So civilised that you use dubious methods to track me down here. You just take care you don't get caught by your own tricks,' Jake said evenly. 'Now go, but if you've any idea about returning or telling others where I am, just remember I know a lot about you which would

85

make good headlines. The media has no loyalty to its own, as you well know.'

When Karl left in a final defiant engine roar, Jake shook Mr Jones' hand.

'Thanks for that.'

As Libby came running towards them, she heard Mr Jones say in wonder, 'I don't know what came over me. I've never threatened anyone in my life except village lads and certainly not with this,' he said, holding up the knife in a shaking hand. 'When Mrs Garfield told me yesterday to keep a close eye on Libby, I wasn't expecting a man like that.'

'He wasn't after her, it was me.' But just as Libby drew level, she thought she heard Jake say in a low voice, 'But Mrs Garfield was right to tell you to keep an eye on Libby.'

'I think we need a cup of tea to calm us all down,' she said a little too brightly.

'Not me,' Mr Jones said, reverting to his normal slight grumpiness. 'I've work to do.'

Libby and Jake exchanged amused glances. 'Thanks, that would be nice,' Jake replied, 'but I'll make it.'

Taking her arm, he steered her towards Oak Lodge and Libby found the contact comforting, reassuring, but as she watched him move efficiently around the small kitchen, for the first time for ages she felt secure.

'A penny for them?' Jake asked, taking the tea bags out of the mugs.

'Oh, I'm sorry you were bothered by that

odious man.'

Would he perhaps say anything about what she had overheard him say to Mr Jones?

'I don't think he'll come again, but just to be sure, don't leave the wood for a few days.'

'Don't leave the wood?' Then with a half laugh she added, 'Why ever not? He's not likely to kidnap one of us, is he?'

'No, not even Karl would be that melodramatic!'

Perched on kitchen stools, sipping their tea, they sat in silence on either side of the counter. But there was something about Jake being so close that had her blurting out, 'Jake, what did Karl really want?'

'Oh, it was nothing really. He's been after me to do some work for him.'

'What sort of work?'

'What I used to do before, but, Libby, if you see anyone at all sneaking around, don't go near them. Come and get me.'

Although she nodded, Libby knew she would have to be very frightened to run for help. It was only later she remembered what she thought Mr Jones had said about Mary telling him to keep an eye on her. Was Jake really telling the truth that Karl was after him? If so, why had Jake been so insistent that she left the carpark? Could it be he was worried Karl would recognise her?

Making the excuse that she had work to do, Libby hurried back to Keeper's Lodge. She had to phone Mary. 'Why did you tell Mr Jones to keep an eye on me?' she demanded as soon as the phone was lifted. 'Surely you're not expecting the media to hunt me out. I'm old news now.'

'Libby, dear, if you give me a chance, I'll try to explain,' Mary soothed. 'I don't think for one moment that you're being hunted. The reason I asked Mr Jones to keep an eye on you was that, despite our precautions, people might try to contact you about the others. Also, I'm a little concerned the men might prove a bit of a handful for you. The artistic temperament is so unpredictable and as they are all at Sanctuary Wood to think things out, they could get a little demanding.'

'So you think I'm not up to the job,' Libby replied hotly.

'If I'd felt that I wouldn't have given it to you. Looking after others is what you're good at.'

'What about Jake?'

'Ah, Jake, now he's a different kettle of fish from the others.'

'In what way? If he's got problems, I should know.'

'That's not possible. Part of the attraction of Sanctuary Wood is anonymity, having privacy to be alone, not be questioned.'

'Mel and Jake seem to know each other well.'

'Libby,' Mary said, more sharply now, 'why

don't you just concentrate on doing your job? Remember, if you start prying, others might feel they can do the same, and are you ready for that?'

Libby sighed deeply, then, 'You're right, of course. I'm sorry.'

'No need to be. Just look after yourself, and the others. If they can't find their own way out of their particular problems, then you might be able to help them. Now I'm sure you've plenty to do.'

It was only as she went into the utility room to tend to the neglected washing machine and tumble dryer, that Libby realised Mary hadn't asked what had happened to make her phone
. . .

'I've brought your laundry back,' Libby called out, dumping Jake's laundry basket on his bench.

Standing back, hands on hips, she looked at the lodge. What was it about buildings that gave them an empty look? Not empty of furniture, but of people?

'Hello!'

This time she knocked loudly on the door. When there was no reply, the irritation she had been feeling bubbled up into annoyance. Unable to face her, he had gone out deliberately! Then a spark of her usual commonsense had her dismissing the idea. Jake was not the sort to avoid her, to hide. So where was he? She couldn't possibly leave it until the evening to ask him if he had phoned Mary, not in front of the others.

Then, thinking she saw someone on the path, she called out, 'Jake! Hi, there!'

But as she ran nimbly through the trees, she realised she had been mistaken. It was Steve.

'Sorry to disappoint you,' he replied, coming towards her and from the way he was smiling, he appeared to be in a very good mood. 'Is it anything I can help you with?' he asked. 'Or do I detect romance in the air? Perhaps after all I shouldn't abandon writing my romances.'

'No, it's nothing like that. Far from it!'

Although Steve made a great show of sighing heavily, his eyes were bright with excitement. 'I was going to thank you this evening. Our little talk really inspired me. My fingers are flying over the keyboard. Well, not actually now they're not. I was just soaking up the atmosphere.'

'Steve, you're not using us as characters, are you? You know the confidentiality Mary insists on, and I'm included in that, too.'

'Of course I haven't used any of you, though Thomas would be good as the possible bad guy.'

'Thomas?' Libby laughed. 'You must see qualities in him that I've missed.'

'Still waters run deep. But seriously, if this place can give him the confidence he needs, then I think that young man will go far. But Mel would make an excellent victim. He's hurt

90

so many people.'

'Hurt? How?'

'Now, now!' Steve wagged a reproving finger at her. 'Remember what you've just said about confidentiality. But we writers are people-watchers and so I've been wondering why a pretty young girl like you shuts herself away from the world with four men, none of whom would stir the female heart, except for Jake, of course,' he said, looking at her intently.

'I wanted to see him about some business,' she said shortly.

'Then go down between Rowan and Birch Lodges. He was down there a few minutes ago, though goodness knows why.'

Jake was indeed where Steve had indicated and even though Libby was some distance away, he turned to face her, but not before she noticed he had been using binoculars to scan the road down which she had first come. Although he was smiling, there was a tenseness about him which curled a knot of anxiety through her. Was he checking whether Karl had really gone?

'Hi, Libby! Looking for me?'

'Did you phone Mary about Karl?' she demanded as she reached him.

'Now why should I do that?' he asked, leaning against a tree trunk, arms folded across his chest, one eyebrow raised in mock enquiry.

'When I phoned her just now, she said something about people trying to contact one of you.'

'Yes, I did phone her. I wanted to know how he knew I was here.'

'How did he know?'

'She doesn't know!'

'Jake, what did he want?' she asked.

'He's gone now, so there's no point in you worrying.'

'So there is something to worry about?' she asked anxiously.

'There's no need to concern yourself. It's me he's after, but I think he got the message.'

'If it's you, then why have you warned me to be careful?'

'Libby, please believe me when I say he came here to see just me. Now if you don't mind, I'd like to get back to my bird watching.'

Although he turned back towards the road and lifted the binoculars, Libby did not believe for one second that he was bird watching.

During the next few days, Libby and the four men settled into a routine which seemed to be to everyone's liking, but although Steve, Mel and Thomas all seemed to be hard at work, Jake was restless, striding through the woods and it seemed to Libby that he passed Keeper's Lodge a dozen times a day. Sometimes he went off on his motorbike, but not for long.

Daily he called in to ask Libby if he could

do shopping, but as Mr Jones now seemed happy to bring groceries and other things, she said there was no need. But what she wanted to ask Jake was why Mr Jones now brought him what looked like a copy of every daily newspaper.

When she had first arrived at Sanctuary Wood, Mr Jones always disappeared into the wood or his shed, so she saw little of him, but now he never seemed to settle at a job. It soon became obvious to Libby that he and Jake had set themselves up as her guardians. But why?

Resentment eventually built up to such a point that when Jake next called in, she exploded. 'Why are you and Mr Jones acting like prison guards? If it isn't you marching about as though on guard, Mr Jones is lurking. Jake, what is going on?'

'I've told you, it really is nothing directly to do with you. It's just that when a man like Karl, who has little scruples, could be hanging about, I can't take chances.'

'What do you mean?' she demanded.

Jake was so good at avoiding a direct answer. He went round in circles until she was mentally dizzy. Well, he was not going to succeed this time!

'You have no right keeping things from me, not when they affect my freedom,'

'Oh, come on, Libby, don't be so dramatic!' he said with a smile.

'Dramatic, am I? I can't move without

either you or your henchman being there.'

'It wasn't me who asked Mr Jones to keep an eye on you, it was Mary.'

Realising this was true, Libby looked away. Then taking a deep, calming breath, she asked, 'Jake, if this man is after you in some way, shouldn't you go to the police?'

'You know what your trouble is, don't you? You've been reading too many of those mystery books you enjoy and so now you're seeing bad guys behind every tree.'

'How do you know what I read?'

'You sometimes leave one on the kitchen table. Perhaps I have overreacted as far as you're concerned, and I'm sorry, but as for Karl, I'm hoping he's got the message.'

'That you want nothing to do with him?'

She glanced up at him enquiringly, but he wouldn't be drawn. 'Look, fancy a spin on my bike? I think Sanctuary Wood is getting us both down a little.'

'That would be fun. I've never been on a motorbike, but I haven't got a helmet or appropriate clothing.'

'I've a spare helmet and as for clothing, just warm things. About ten minutes?' he said, turning to leave.

CHAPTER TEN

Because it was Libby's first time on a motorbike, Jake deliberately went slowly down the track to the road, but once there, he wanted to increase the speed, but what Jake did not realise was this was the first time Libby had been so close to a man since Grant had died. She knew it was illogical but she was apprehensive.

'Libby, if you're that nervous about being on a bike, we'll go back.'

'No, I'm not nervous. It's just that it takes a little getting used to.'

Suddenly the tension left her, but she was unaware she was leaning forward, head resting on his back, arms more firmly around his body. Although Jake also relaxed, he increased his speed slowly. When he asked if she was all right, she lifted her head to reply but in doing so, realised she had been almost cuddling him! What must he think of her!

When she felt the bike slow, then stop, she jerked away from him, tense again. He was silent as he helped her off, his helmet visor still down so she could not see his expression. Sudden panic had her ripping off her helmet, gasping for air.

'Libby, what is it?' Lifting his visor, the worry in his eyes matched his voice. 'What

95

memories have been resurrected? For sure they're not good ones.'

'I told you, I've not been on a bike before.'

She looked down, fiddling with the chin strap of her helmet.

'Then it was the closeness to me,' he said flatly.

'No! It wasn't you. It was just . . .'

His helmet off now, he slowly put it on the bike seat. 'Libby, I would never do anything to hurt you.'

Although she nodded, she still avoided looking at him. Taking her helmet and his, he opened the field gate near which they had stopped. 'There's a river over there, let's take a walk.'

As he shut the gate behind them, she said just a little too brightly, 'How do you know about the river? I can't see it.'

'An old habit. I always check my surroundings.'

Grant used to say that, too! She had to stop Grant's name popping into her head, so hurriedly she said, 'I realise to my shame that although I love the country I don't really see things properly.'

'Besides always checking a map, I look for tell-tale signs, like those willow trees,' he said, pointing. 'They always grow by water, and as we are in a valley, there's generally a stream or river in it.'

Then, stopping and dropping the helmets,

he took hold of her arm as he pointed to distant smoke billowing from the depths of Sanctuary Wood. 'And Mr Jones is burning tree prunings and they're fresh.'

'How do you know that?'

She wanted to keep his attention on the wood, keep his hand on her arm.

'If the wood was dry, it wouldn't burn with so much smoke. I'm surprised he hasn't left it to stand, dry out a little.'

Turning to face her, his hand went from her arm to cradle her chin. Grey eyes met and held hers.

She didn't realise she was frowning until his hand went to gently ease away the furrows, nor did she realise she had closed her eyes, was holding her breath. His lips brushed hers in a kiss so fleeting that she wondered if she had been mistaken. Opening her eyes, she saw he was looking at her questioningly.

'Was that wrong of me?' he asked softly.

As his breath fanned her face, she struggled to find words which would express her whirling emotions.

'Sorry,' he said, gruffly. He was already walking stiff-backed towards the gate. Hurrying to catch him up, they were both silent as they went back to the bike and returned to Sanctuary Wood.

'Thank you,' Libby said stiffly, handing him her helmet. Then feeling more than a little responsible for the unease between them she

97

added, 'I enjoyed it.'

'The bike ride?'

Jake wasn't there for the evening meal and predictably, Mel complained about the smoke from the bonfire. When he did, Steve smiled.

'What's so funny?' Mel said, helping himself to the lasagne she had made. 'You wouldn't notice if you were sitting on top of the blazing heap.'

'You'd better be careful. Perhaps Steve is writing you into his plot,' Thomas teased.

Then as though remembering what he considered to be his lowly place, he looked down at his plate. 'Perhaps I've already written him in,' Steve said blandly.

'I'm not having you putting me in one of your books. If you do, I'll sue!'

'Oh, stop it will you!' Libby snapped and they were all so astonished that for a few minutes they restricted themselves to polite comments about passing plates and glasses.

'Thomas,' Libby said to break the oppressive silence, 'how is your music going? Don't forget you promised to play for us one evening.'

When he replied eagerly that his composing was going well, Libby's gentle questioning soon had him explaining the basics of composition. His enthusiasm was so infectious that even Mel and Steve joined in and over coffee it was agreed he would play for them the following evening.

'Let's make it a party!' Steve said. 'Libby, you can have a rest from slaving for us. I'll do the food. About the only thing I'm good at in the kitchen is fancy nibbles. But as the cooking area in the lodges is so small, can I borrow your kitchen?'

This unexpected relief from routine seemed to please everyone and as the three men seemed happy to take over all of the arrangements, Libby sat back, smiling slightly as though she was listening and agreeing. But her thoughts were on Jake and the last words he had said to her as they had parted that afternoon.

'I think I'd better give this evening a miss, for both our sakes.'

The arrangements sorted out to everyone's satisfaction, Thomas and Mel left, the latter with his arm around the musician. Steve stood for a moment on the veranda, looking up at the few stars visible through the trees.

'It's a lovely night,' Libby said.

'Yes, I'm almost sorry I've given up writing romances,' he sighed in mock sorrow. 'But talking about romance, I can't think of another way of broaching the subject, Libby, you and Jake need to be careful.'

'Careful?' she repeated. 'Of what?'

'In very different ways, you're both very vulnerable. With my romantic novelist's hat on, I would like to see you both living happily ever after, but two injured hearts don't necessarily mend together.' Then giving her a swift kiss on the cheek, he said, 'Just listen to me! I'd better get back to my mystery before I decide to use you and Jake as the main characters in a romance.'

The beautiful night suddenly bringing a lump to her throat, Libby closed the curtains and lit the log-burning stove. When it was radiating a comforting warmth, she curled up in the armchair, hugging a cushion for comfort.

But then Steve's warning came back to her about two injured hearts. What did he know about Jake?

Sleep did not bring any answers to how Libby should tackle Jake, but just as she was pouring water into the coffee percolator next morning, he tapped lightly on the window.

Unlocking the door, she made herself smile at him. If she behaved as though nothing had happened, then perhaps he would realise that yesterday was of no consequence.

'I'm sorry it's early. But I want to explain. Can I come in?'

Leaving the door open, she went back into the kitchen. 'Coffee?' she called back over her shoulder.

'Yes, thanks.'

'Come in,' she said, not looking at him. 'You can sit there if you like,' she added, pointing to one of the high stools.

When he didn't move, she turned sharply,

unsmiling as she said, 'Jake, I would have invited the others to sit down, and you're no . . .'

'Different to them,' he finished heavily.

Sitting down, he rested tightly-clasped hands on the counter.

'Thomas is going to play for us tonight,' she said brightly, but her eyes were fixed on the percolating coffee. 'I'm sure he'd want you there.'

'But do you?'

Having sensed that he had moved, she guessed he was looking at her. 'Of course I do! Why shouldn't I?'

'It wouldn't be surprising after yesterday.'

'Oh, that!' she said dismissively, going to fetch milk. 'It was only a peck.'

Glancing at him, she saw his jaw tighten. 'I'm glad you see it that way,' he replied stiffly.

When he looked as though he was getting up, she felt the need to stop him. She hadn't meant to hurt him. 'Jake, I'm sorry.'

'You can't help how you feel. I should have realised you might still want to keep all men at arm's length. But honestly, Libby, it came as much of a surprise to me as it did to you.'

'Because you still haven't got over whatever happened between you and Mel to do with your girlfriend.'

'She was beautiful.'

Libby sighed. No-one had ever called her that, not even Grant when he was trying to get

101

her to go somewhere she didn't want to go. His silver tongue didn't stretch to that lie!

'He persuaded her to sit for him. Mel can never resist a beautiful woman.'

'Then I'm safe from him!'

'I thought she would see him for what he was, a womaniser, but she didn't.'

'The pink envelopes?'

'They're not her style and anyway, he dumped her months ago. A footballer's wife took his eye.'

'Won't she come back to you?'

Although he answered almost immediately, it seemed to Libby like hours. 'No, we've both moved on, are different people.'

'In that case, why do you still harbour a grudge against Mel? That's not moving on, is it?'

'And have you moved on?'

Leaning forward, he hooked the fine gold chain out of its hiding place beneath her top, but as her hand clutched her wedding ring, he let go.

'It means that much to you, does it?' he asked. 'I'm sorry, I shouldn't have taken advantage.'

'You didn't take advantage. A kiss hardly merits that. And as for this . . .' Bending her head, she slipped the chain off, then held it in her hand.

'Don't do that, unless you're really ready to move on,' he said softly.

Staring at the ring, remembering, the good times, for it hadn't all been bad, she nodded. She was indeed ready.

Jake had left suddenly, without a word. Letting the fine chain run through her fingers, she wondered if this was because he wanted to give her time to really consider if now was the time to put away Grant's ring.

Going into the living-room, she slipped the chain and ring into the little silver trinket box which Grant had given her. It seemed right they should be together.

Remembering Mel having reported a tap was dripping in his wash basin, Libby was on the lookout for Mr Jones to ask him to see to it.

Libby was snapped out of her thoughts by Mr Jones declaring behind her, 'Waste of time cleaning windows. Birds will use them for target practice, clean or not.'

'You gave me a fright! I never heard you coming.'

'Country folk don't go crashing about,' he said. 'I just met that there man who wears bright shirts. He was driving his car as though a swarm of bees was after him. It's a good job there was a verge for me to swerve on to. And that lad down in Birch, he's quiet enough in himself but to me that noise he makes isn't music.'

'Perhaps it's a good thing we all have different tastes in music and books,' Libby interrupted. 'Mr Jones, before you start outside work, could you fix a dripping tap in Spruce?'

'I suppose I must,' he muttered. 'But if that there Mel fellow tells me how to do my job . . .'

'I doubt he will. I get the impression he doesn't know one end of a screwdriver from the other,' Libby said, going to the door.

It was mid-afternoon when Steve arrived with several carrier bags, the name on them indicating he had not been to Priorbury, but an expensive grocer in the nearest town.

Helping him carry the bags into the kitchen, Libby smiled. Steve's liking for food was obvious from his rotund figure and the way he enjoyed her cooking, but the carriers also indicated he was a gourmet. Although she offered to unpack and store perishables in the fridge, he insisted he would do it, coming back in the early evening to put out the food.

Steve was just trying to fit a large quantity of smoked salmon into the fridge, when Mr Jones burst in.

'What happened?' Libby sighed. 'What has Mel said to upset you now?'

'He's given me this list. Said I'd have to go and buy this wine. I told him running errands weren't part of my job but then he had the nerve to try to give me money as though I were an errand boy!'

'Oh, sorry, that might be my fault,' Steve said ruefully. 'He asked me to get it, but I told him to get it himself.'

Before Libby could say anything, Steve went on to explain that they were preparing the evening meal as a treat for Libby and hearing this Mr Jones grudgingly agreed to get the wine.

'Thanks for that,' Libby said, as Mr Jones left. 'But I wasn't expecting such a lavish spread and as for the wine, I do have some here.'

'Mel wasn't to be outdone by me. He knows I like good food so you watch, he'll have sent for the most expensive wine. But I must go. I've a mystery that wants solving.'

Realising the furniture in the living-room would have to be rearranged so they could all sit comfortably to listen to Thomas, Libby was just wondering where he would like to put his keyboard, when there was a knock on the door.

Thinking it was Mr Jones returning with the wine, she called out, 'Put them in the kitchen. I'll see to them in a minute.'

As she heard cupboard doors being opened and closed, then a tap running, she hurried to see what was happening.

'Jake! I thought you were someone else. Mel sent Mr Jones to get wine.'

'I know. I met him in the village and he told me all about it. But don't worry, a drink in the pub soothed him, especially when I said I'd bring the wine. I hope you don't mind, but I also told him to take the rest of the day off. He needed it after a dose of Mel.'

'No, I don't mind. But what are you looking for? Shouldn't the wine be cooling?'

'I'll see to that in a minute. I was looking for that jug you used for my sad lilies the other day, but I think it will be too large. Steve is very bossy when he puts his mind to it and he ordered me to get flowers for this evening. You'll be glad to know, I've done a little better this time, but although I put them very carefully into the bike panniers, they are still looking a little sad.'

Going out on to the veranda, Jake returned carrying a large bunch of lily of-the-valley.

'Oh, they're beautiful,' Libby exclaimed. 'Their scent is wonderful, one of my favourites. But you're right, the jug is too big, but I've lots of glasses. We could dot them around here and in the living-room.'

As she took the flowers from him, Libby realised they were not tied in bunches but had damp kitchen paper around them.

'Where did you get these?' she asked.

'When I walked back here the other day after taking my bike into the garage, I noticed that the old cottage by the church had a whole drift of them. So today I asked if I could have some. When I told her why, the old woman who lives there insisted I had all of these. Wouldn't be paid either, but she asked me to take you to see her one day.'

As Libby arranged the flowers in several glasses, Jake watched her. 'Do you know about the language of flowers?' he asked eventually.

'Oh, you mean red roses for love?'

She felt safe saying it, for he hadn't given her roses.

'The old woman told me lily-of-the-valley means return of happiness. I hope it will indeed be true for you.'

Taken aback by the floral message, Libby could only mutter an awkward, 'Thank you.'

'Libby,' but Jake got no further for loud, happy exchanges between Steve and Thomas made it obvious the two were coming with the latter's keyboard.

Glad of the excuse, Libby hurried to open the door and hoped that her smile was normal, for Steve, besides being observant, seemed to be able to sense the atmosphere.

Soon all four of them were in Libby's living-room, discussing the best place for the keyboard, then arranging seating. This done, Thomas wanted to rehearse, saying he needed to get used to the room's acoustics.

'Stay as long as you like,' Libby encouraged, avoiding looking at Jake.

She knew he would have guessed that she didn't want to resume their conversation, and didn't want to see his questioning look.

'Jake,' Steve said, 'have you time to come back with me to Rowan? I need some expert advice on photography. I can see I've a lot to learn about the nuts and bolts of writing a mystery. Sooner or later I'm going to have to find a friendly policeman to guide me through some of the detective work.'

'Libby, are you all right?' Jake asked.

To the other two it seemed like a normal polite question about her needing more help but she knew he meant his comment about the lily-of-the-valley.

Although she was pleased to see Thomas so enthusiastic about his music, after a while, his repeated rehearsing of the same few bars as he strove for perfection got on her nerves. When she told him she was going for a walk and to help himself to a drink or make a sandwich when he was hungry, he just nodded vaguely.

Going across the carpark and through the gate, she began walking down the track to the road. She failed to see the man who had been watching from the edge of the wood.

'Hi, Libby!'

She spun round, hand to her chest in fright but when she saw it was Karl, fright turned into annoyance. 'Jake said he didn't want to see you,' she reminded sharply.

'He'll soon change his mind when he gets bored with all of this,' he said, waving a contemptuous hand towards the fields and wood.

'Then why are you hanging about?'

'Waiting for Jake to change his mind.'

'If he does, I'm sure he'll contact you,' she

said, surprised at the steadiness of her own voice. 'So there's no point in you hanging about.'

He was looking at her so intently, she shivered. There was something very threatening about him.

'Well, you might have time to hang about, but I haven't,' she said.

She wanted to run back to Sanctuary Wood, but resisted the urge. She didn't want Karl to think for even one second that he was scaring her.

'As this isn't private, I'll walk back with you as far as the gate,' he said smoothly. 'And you can tell me all about your little secret retreat.'

'If you're that interested, you can get a brochure.'

'Have we met before?' His question hitting her like a blow, she stopped.

'I don't think so,' she said, forcing herself to look him in the eye.

Head on one side, he was looking at her through eyes narrowed by concentration. Had he guessed who she was?

Libby heard the distinctive sound of Mr Jones' battered van before Karl and this gave her courage, 'If I'd met someone as unpleasant as you before, I would most certainly have remembered,' she said. Then moving off the track, she added, 'If you don't want to get run over, I suggest you leave. Mr Jones isn't very good at steering that old van of his. And you have met him before. He was the one with the pruning knife.'

Muttering about senile old men, Karl hurried away, breaking into a run as Mr Jones blared his horn.

Drawing up by Libby, Mr Jones leaned out of his window and asked with obvious delight, 'Shall I chase him?'

'No! Leave him, but thanks. You came at just the right time. But why are you here? I thought Jake had brought back the wine.'

'He did, but I wanted to check on that dripping tap, see it's all right. Jump in and I'll give you a lift back.'

Although the wood was only a short distance away, Libby complied. She doubted Karl would have lingered, but she desperately wanted to get back to Sanctuary Wood. She suddenly needed the security it offered.

Having insisted on seeing Libby safely into Keeper's Lodge, Mr Jones surprisingly refused a cup of tea and a biscuit, muttering he had something to see to. Although part of her would have liked to be alone to calm down and think about the meeting with Karl, Libby was glad of Thomas's company, even though he was still at the keyboard. Realising he still hadn't stopped for even a drink, she was just making him a cheese and tomato sandwich when Jake thrust open the door.

'What do you mean going off by yourself like that?' he demanded angrily.

Taking hold of her by the shoulders, his anger was so apparent that she tried to shrink away. 'What did I tell you? If you wanted to go out, I would have taken you.'

His anger, combined with the lingering unease of Karl's questioning was too much for her self-control. Sobbing, she went limp, leaning against Jake's chest. Momentarily he stiffened, but then, one arm around her, he stroked her hair. 'There, it's all right. I'm sorry I shouted, but I don't want Karl to even suspect who you are. He's unscrupulous.'

Leaning his face against her head, Jake made inconsequential noises as though comforting a child. Slowly, Libby's sobs subsided and it was then she really became aware of their closeness, the comfort of his arms, his whispered words.

Kissing the top of her head, Jake said softly. 'Come and sit down. You need a cup of sweet tea.'

No! She didn't want tea! She wanted to stay in his arms! But he was leading her into the living-room, guiding her gently to the settee. 'I'm sorry. I shouldn't have gone. But I never thought that man would still be about.'

'Neither did I,' Jake said grimly, sitting down beside her.

'Where's Thomas?' she asked, peering around as though he might be hiding.

'I think he saw us. Do you mind?'

She shook her head. Then before Jake

could follow up with another searching question she asked, 'How did you know Karl had been here?'

'Mr Jones told me. He came back because he'd heard Karl had been asking questions in the village pub. Luckily he was just in time to scare him off. I owe you an explanation about Karl. He was my agent. He and I seemed to share the same ideas, but when he saw what large sums of money were handed out by the newspapers who thought more about circulation than what was right, he changed. He would have sold what happened between Mel and me if he could, but at the time he had just enough loyalty to me not to.'

'But he hasn't now?' she asked.

'What happened with Mel and me is past history. He wants me to . . .'

But Jake got no further for Steve came hurrying in.

'What's this I hear from Thomas about Libby being in tears?'

'Karl's been snooping,' Jake explained. 'Gave Libby a fright.'

'He hasn't been after her, has he?' Steve was obviously worried.

'Not now, Steve.'

There was a warning in Jake's voice which had Libby looking at him searchingly but the scene suddenly switched so suddenly that she shook her head as though coming out of a dream.

'Of course, you're right,' Steve was saying. 'We've a musical soiree to get ready for. Libby, is it all right if I get going in the kitchen? I'm starving! What do you think would be best? Food first, or after Thomas has played?'

Feeling disorientated as though she was both part of a play, but yet watching it, Libby began to stand up. When she seemed to be a little unsteady, Jake swiftly put his arm around her.

'Look, why don't you go and shower? I'll help Steve.' Giving her a gentle push, Jake smiled.

Libby sighed as she opened her bedroom door. It was then she saw the box on the bed. How had it got there? Picking it up, she recognised Mary's handwriting. Mary had only e-mailed the previous evening, so why hadn't she mentioned the parcel then?

CHAPTER ELEVEN

Opening the box carefully, Libby gasped with astonishment. Then she lifted out the fine fabric. The dress was mid-calf, thin straps holding up the top which, as she held it up in front of her, she knew was an exact fit, without being revealing. That would never do with four men about! But why had Mary sent it? How had she known about the special evening?

Puzzled, she looked in the box for a card or letter. The envelope was small. Libby opened it.

I was asked to buy you this specific frock. Hope it fits! Enjoy the evening, Mary.

If Mary had thought the mystery would excite Libby, she was wrong. Libby found it strangely upsetting for who knew where she was, and about the evening? Turning the card over as though in a moment of mischief Mary might have written the giver's name on the back, Libby realised it could only have been one of the four men. But which one? Certainly not Thomas, but could it be Steve, echoes of his romantic novel writing still lingering? But from the garish shirts he always wore, he wouldn't have been attracted to such subtle shades. That pointed to an artist's eye . . . surely not Mel!

'Libby, is everything all right?' Jake's enquiry immediately cleared her thoughts. If he had been worried about her, wouldn't he have said, 'Are you all right?'

It must be Jake! It had to be him. Picking up the dress, she opened the door.

'Do you know anything about this?' she asked, eyes sparkling.

'Guilty!' he said ruefully. 'I hope you don't mind but I guessed you wouldn't have brought anything other than practical clothes.'

She didn't meet his eyes, couldn't, but instead seemed intent on moving the frock slightly so the filmy fabric floated out.

'Go and shower then let me see if my hunch was right, that it is just perfect for you,' Jake said.

'Do the others know?' she asked.

She looked up at him, wanting to see his expression. She really didn't need his answer for the look in his eyes told her it was his gift alone.

'Perhaps it would be better if the others didn't know?' he asked.

She looked away. There was so much behind that seemingly innocent question. If the others knew, they might jump to the wrong conclusions. 'How did you arrange it with Mary, tell her which one to buy?'

'I had to go to town and when I saw this in a shop window, I thought of you. But I didn't know your size, or quite have enough nerve to go in and buy it. Mary's great isn't she? Pity Grant . . .'

Reaching up, she stopped him by placing her finger on his mouth, 'I really don't want to hear his name, not tonight. Everyone has made such an effort, I'm sure it's going to be wonderful.'

Libby had often felt self-conscious when Grant had insisted she wear clothes which were too eye-catching for her taste, but trying to see herself in the small mirror on the bedroom wall, she knew the dress was indeed perfect. It fitted without revealing, was delicate without seeming unsuitable for the occasion.

'Come on, Libby!' Steve shouted. 'We're all dying to see you.'

'Don't say that!' she heard Thomas say with far more authority than she had ever heard him use. 'You'll embarrass her.'

'How do you know that?' Mel, too, was in the living-room. 'I think you're not as inexperienced about girls as you would have us believe.'

'I'm guessing,' was his hurried reply. 'I hate being the centre of attention and I guess Libby does, too.'

Libby tried to walk into the living-room as though it was an everyday occurrence for her to be dressed so glamorously.

'I have got to paint you in that!' Mel was the first to react. 'Even if Jake does challenge me to pistols at dawn.'

Startled, she looked up at the half circle of admiring men, Mel, Steve and Thomas. But where was Jake? Coming up to kiss her hand, Steve whispered, 'He won't be long. Said he had to get something.'

'Now, if I was to do that and Jake caught me,' Mel complained but good-humouredly, 'I really would be in trouble.' Then turning to Thomas, he teased gently, 'I guess you're too young to be kissing a young lady's hand.'

As Thomas reddened, Mel continued, 'Libby, I think you've made yet another

116

conquest.'

'Thomas, like a true artist, thinks only of his work, don't you?' She smiled at him.

'Ouch!' Mel said in mock pain. 'That's just the sort of thing Jake would say to me!'

But Libby suggested they sit down and Thomas could play for them until Jake returned. Although they had been expecting some of his own compositions, he began with The Moonlight Sonata, a good choice, for it relaxed them. But she wasn't as relaxed as she seemed, for she was wondering where Jake was, and what he was bringing.

He came in so quietly she was unaware until the settee moved slightly under his weight.

'Jake, you gave me a fright,' she said quietly. Leaning towards her, he whispered, 'You're beautiful!'

Libby turned to him but when she saw his face so near hers, his eyes on her lips, she leaned farther away. A quick glance told her that both Steve and Mel were watching, smiling.

'Come on everyone, interval time!' Steve ordered, standing up. 'Thomas, we all enjoyed that, more later, I hope. Libby, you're to be a lady of leisure and so stay here until we fetch you.'

Hurrying into the kitchen, he fussed about uncovering dishes and plates, whilst directing Thomas and Mel to fetch wine and food which had been in the fridge. He then lit the numerous small candles which he had dotted about the room.

'Libby, can we go into the office?' Jake asked, offering his hand to help her up. 'It's a little more private.'

Although she really didn't need it, she accepted his help, enjoying the feeling of being cosseted, looked after.

'I wanted to show you these, see what you think.'

He still had on his leather jacket and, unzipping it slightly, withdrew a large envelope. As he took out coloured photographs, he handed them to her.

Conscious her opinion seemed to matter to him, Libby studied each one intently. They were all of country scenes, landscapes, moss on a damp stone, the shadow of trees on a sunny bank and a slightly blurred one of a blackbird.

'I'm used to taking action pictures in war zones, so you'd think I'd manage a blackbird just about to take off. But as you can see, I've a lot to learn.'

Going back to one particular photograph, Libby put her head on one side as she tried to find the right words. 'I do like this one. The ray of sunlight illuminating that clump of bluebells . . . it's . . . well, I think it's wonderful!'

'I liked that one, too. By the way, do you know what the bluebell signifies? It's constancy. Libby, I do hope you find a partner who is truly constant, who doesn't let you down.'

He was looking at her with such tenderness that Libby eyes filled with tears. But they were not of sadness, for what might have been with Grant, but with a longing of what the future might hold. But when Jake bent to kiss her, Libby had turned away to wipe away spilling tears. She mustn't cry!

'You two!' Steve was shouting from the kitchen. 'We're waiting for you.'

'Shall we?' Jake said, formally offering her his arm.

When she touched her face, checking for tears, Jake took her hand away and kissed it. 'I wanted to do that to your tears, but perhaps I caused them, so had no right.'

Shaking her head, Libby slipped her arm through his, leaving him wondering whether her head shake had been that she did not want his kisses, or that he did have the right.

Holding tightly to this last thought, he brought his arm close to his body, wanting to feel her against him. She sighed, fleetingly leaning her head again at his arm.

'Come on, let's face them,' Jake encouraged. 'They'll be too busy eating to notice us.'

But as they went in, Mel exclaimed, 'My goodness, look at you! A bridal pair if ever I saw one.'

Seeing Libby's embarrassment, and thinking

119

how he would feel in such circumstances, Thomas took a plate and handed it to Libby. 'Come on,' he encouraged. 'I'm starving and we can't start before the guest of honour!'

As Jake reluctantly released her, Libby dared not look at him, not with three pairs of watchful eyes on them. But as Thomas acted as her escort, seeing her plate was filled, steering her to a seat, it was now Jake's turn to watch and he did so with barely concealed irritation.

'Look, champagne!' Thomas exclaimed. 'Is Mel celebrating something?'

'Gentlemen,' Mel's slight smile belied his pompous tone. 'A toast to Libby!' Then turning to her continued with unusual gentleness, 'I, we, owe so much to you. Thomas has, I think, made a good start on what I'm sure will be a brilliant career. Steve, well, I hope you've not made me the villain of your new book.'

'How did you know what I was writing?' Steve demanded.

'I've seen you pacing about the wood, miming falls, hiding behind trees as though shadowing someone. I, too, have been doing the previously unthinkable, walking a little! I have attempted a few watercolours, you know the sort of thing which appeal to the romantic.'

'I haven't seen you in the woods.' Jake frowned.

'You were too busy creeping about with

120

your camera and anyway, I don't wear bright shirts like someone I could mention.'

Everyone laughed, except Jake, and as Libby risked a quick glance in his direction, she saw he was looking down into his glass as though it was a crystal ball.

'What about Libby herself?' His question stilled the laughter, brought all the attention on to her. 'I hope you've found what you were looking for, but I doubt we've been of much help. Being so bound up with our own problems. We've taken you for granted.'

Tears threatening to spill over again. Libby interrupted hastily with, 'I was just doing my job. But come on, let's enjoy this wonderful feast and champagne, then Thomas's music.'

CHAPTER TWELVE

Waking the following morning, Libby's hand went to her throbbing head. Unused to drinking much alcohol, she'd had three glasses of champagne. Lying in bed, the other arm across her eyes to shield from the bright morning light, she fought through the fuzz, trying to remember what had happened, but she could only recall disjointed snatches. Eating the wonderful food . . . Mel trying to pour her more champagne, and when she tried to refuse, Thomas coming to her rescue. But where had Jake been?

She frowned, groaning as this small movement made her headache worse. He was dimly in the shadows, avoiding her, but watchful, then when Thomas played again, Jake hadn't sat with her. It had been Steve beside her on the settee, Steve who bent to whisper how much he was enjoying the music. Glancing up, she had caught Jake looking at her, jaw set. Could he, she wondered, have been jealous.

Grant had been jealous! Oh, she didn't want Jake to be like him! Getting out of bed very cautiously, Libby concentrated on showering for several minutes. Then wrapping a large towel around her like a sarong, she sat on the edge of her bed to towel her hair.

Dressing, she decided to give breakfast a miss. She needed to think and walking through the woods might help her brain to work. She took a little-used path which led downhill away from the lodges. For several minutes she had to concentrate on her footing, for the path was unclear, brambles, and small trees impeding her way.

'Libby, it's me.'

'Jake, talk of the devil!' she exclaimed.

He was coming up slowly towards her, using a large stick to clear the way.

She wanted to run away, but why? She certainly wasn't frightened of him physically, but she was frightened about what he might say . . . she might say.

Reaching her, he stopped a couple of paces away as though giving her room to move, to evade him if she wanted to.

'Which way did you come?' she asked, trying to sound casual.

'Oh, I've walked right round the boundary. Mr Jones keeps it clear so he can see when fences need mending.'

He was still slightly below her, looking up, but Libby gazed over his head as though entranced by the hill opposite. Taking a deep breath, he squared his shoulders as though coming to a momentous decision. 'Libby, yesterday evening, I wanted you all to myself. I didn't want to share you with the others. I wanted to talk, tell you . . .'

'You could have stayed after the others had gone.'

He shook his head. 'I might have wanted them gone, but without them there . . . Can we talk? There's a fallen log near the fence.'

He had wanted to be with her! She could have shouted with joy, but when she looked at him, he was frowning.

He offered his hand to help her down to the log and when she took it, she tried to gauge whether his hold was that of concern or of love.

'Libby there's so much I want to say to you.' Pausing he sighed, as though unsure where to begin. 'But first I must explain why I came here, even though it might change things.'

'Go on, I'm listening,' she encouraged softly.

'Grant and I saw many of the same things,' he began slowly. 'You loved him. I don't want you to despise me.'

'Why should I? That I once loved Grant has nothing to do with anything you might tell me.'

'Libby, I'm a coward!'

It was said so quickly, she wondered if she had heard correctly, but a quick glance at his face told her she had. 'Go on,' she said evenly. 'Tell me. I need to know. Grant never shared things with me. It was as though I was there purely for decoration, to boost his ego.'

'He did love you, he must have done. But perhaps he seemed shallow, uncaring, because like me, he had seen so many terrible things. Perhaps his way of dealing with it all was to erect a high wall around himself.'

'Which excluded me,' she said slowly.

Why hadn't she realised Grant might have been affected by what he wrote about? Reading about it was bad enough, but to actually see . . .

'I wasn't a very good wife,' she said sadly. 'I never asked him to tell me any details.'

'He wouldn't have said anything. The life you led together, parties, it was his way of coping.'

'But I should have realised.'

'You were very young, inexperienced,' he

reminded her. His hand had curled so tightly around hers that she nearly cried out.

'You must have seen some of the pictures I took, even if you didn't realise they were mine. But there were many which couldn't be printed. I know dreadful things shouldn't be pushed away, hidden, but I knew I had reached the point when I either built an excluding wall, or backed off.'

'You are not a coward!' she said firmly. 'And how do you know Grant might not have given up at some time?'

Then she remembered Karl. 'Was Karl trying to get you to go back?'

He nodded. 'I was good at it. Good at taking pictures of dreadful things. What a way to be remembered!'

'But you needn't be remembered just for that. I saw those other photographs last night. They were good. People need to be shown there's beauty, too,' she said, putting her other hand on top of his. 'But, Karl, were you frightened he would recognise me?'

'When Mary realised he was trying to find me, she knew he might see you. That's when she told Mr Jones to keep an eye on you. I told her I'd leave here, but she insisted I stay. She said you needed me.'

'I'll always be grateful to her. She seems to have a remarkable way of knowing just what is right for me. I sometimes wonder if she set up Sanctuary Wood more for me than for you lot.'

Letting go of her hand, he took hold of her shoulders, turning her more towards him, so he could see her eyes, the mirror of all emotions.

'And do you?' he demanded. 'Do you need me?'

Her reply was to kiss him gently, but as soon as he felt her lips on his, he pulled her closer, kissing her with an urgency which had her responding eagerly.

It was Jake who heard the camera shutter's characteristic sound, slight though it was. Angrily he stood up and, caught by surprise, Libby toppled over the back of the log.

'What a shot!' a gleeful voice exclaimed. 'Bowled over by Lover Boy's kisses.'

'Karl, give me that camera!' Jake yelled.

But Karl was already running down a field to the road where a car was waiting. He hadn't reckoned on Jake's speed. Getting shakily to her feet, Libby watched aghast as Jake vaulted over the fence. He brought Karl down with a rugby tackle.

'Give it to me!' Jake ordered through clenched teeth.

But Karl was not about to give in so easily. A newspaper would pay handsomely for pictures of Grant's young widow in a clinch!

Hand over her mouth in horror, Libby watched as the two men tussled, rolling down the slope, first one on top, then the other. Several blasts from the horn of the waiting car startled Karl. This gave Jake just the opportunity he wanted.

'Got it!' he yelled, holding up the camera.

Knees either side of his gasping opponent, he tore out the film, holding it aloft victoriously like a flag. Then getting up, he threw down the camera.

'Karl, I never would have believed you would stoop so low, but money often shows people in their true colours.'

'You'll regret this!' Karl shouted over his shoulder as he hurried away. 'I can still sell the story.'

'Jake!' Libby implored. 'Let him go.'

The sob in her voice brought him running to her. Catching her and holding her close, he said, 'I'm sorry I got you into this mess. By tomorrow Karl's story will be all over the more sensational papers, even though he hasn't pictures.'

'I don't care!' she declared. 'I don't care if the whole world knows.'

Holding her away, he looked at her searchingly for a few seconds.

'You really don't care, do you? I can't believe it. You love me! But we can't stay here. There will be others who will try for photographs. Libby, come away with me, to Gretna Green.'

'But Steve, Mel and Thomas . . . I can't leave them. They won't be able to manage.'

'Yes, we will!' three voices chorused. Having

heard the car horn, they had come running and were now standing a few metres away, smiling.

'Is it far to Gretna Green?' she asked Jake softly. 'Scotland would be a lovely place to start your new career and our life together.'